BURIED TREASURES
OF
CALIFORNIA

Buried Treasures of California

Legends from California's Mountains, Deserts, Beaches, and Cities

W.C. Jameson

August House Publishers, Inc.
LITTLE ROCK

Published 1995 by August House, Inc.,
P.O. Box 3223, Little Rock, Arkansas, 72203,
501-372-5450.

Printed in the United States of America

10 9 8 7 6 5 4 3 2 1 PB

LIBRARY OF CONGRESS CATALOGING-IN-PUBLICATION DATA
Buried Treasures of California / W.C. Jameson.
p.   cm.
Includes bibliographical references
ISBN 0-87483-406-6 : $10.95
1. Treasure-trove—California—Folklore.
2. Tales—California. 3. Legends—California.
I. Title.
GR110.C3J36   1995
398.2'09794'06—dc20   94-42466

Executive editor: Liz Parkhurst
Project editor: Rufus Griscom
Design director: Ted Parkhurst
Cover art and map design: Wendell E. Hall

The paper used in this publication meets the minimum requirements of
the American National Standard for Information Sciences—Permanence of
Paper for Printed Library Materials, ANSI Z39.48-1984.

AUGUST HOUSE, INC.   PUBLISHERS   LITTLE ROCK

To Fred Bean
for la buen amistad

Contents

Introduction

CALIFORNIA IS AN EXTRAORDINARY PLACE. It contains huge, bustling cities as well as spectacular and remote wilderness. It offers a variety of landscapes and climates, ranging from glacially-capped mountain peaks to wind-swept and arid deserts to the sea-washed coastline. It has been said that California contains a greater variety of people than any other state.

California is also endowed with an almost limitless supply of precious ore, discovered and undiscovered, priceless metals formed in the ground that inspired early Spanish explorations, the Gold Rush of 1849, and an incredible legacy of folktales, legends, and mythology of lost mines and buried treasures.

In many ways, the state of California reflects, historically and culturally, the settlement of the American West. Initially a relatively remote and isolated region inhabited only by Indians, California's coast, mountains, and deserts were explored and subsequently settled in selected areas by early voyagers, most of them Spanish. Like many other western states, California offers a remarkable diversity of geological regions, each contributing to the natural resources of the area, mineral and otherwise. These resources were coveted by newcomers, and the subsequent discovery and extraction of precious metals attracted others to the area. The arrival of thousands, lured by the promise of mineral wealth, land, and assorted business opportunities, led to a meeting and mixing of cultures—American Indian, Anglo, and Spanish initially, and later others such as Irish and Chinese—and proved to be a remarkable catalyst for progress, settlement, occasional dispute and conflict, and the generation and proliferation of some remarkable tales of the search, discovery, and sometimes eventual loss of many gold mines and hidden caches of magnificent treasures.

THE LAND

The state of California is geologically unique among all of the United States because it is located on two separate continental plates, each moving, grinding, and bumping against the other in a series of tectonic episodes that sometimes cause earthquakes. As California became settled and large cities and towns sprang up, earthquakes occasionally ravaged the communities, causing millions of dollars in damages and incredible loss of life. But the shifting of the earth also accounted for other aspects of the California environment—the creation of impressive mountain ranges and the development of some of the harshest and most forbidding deserts in the world.

The convergence of the enormous continental plates caused great portions of the earth's crust to fold and elevate to altitudes of several thousand feet above sea level. Newly exposed in this massive upheaval of Plutonic granites were seams and veins of gold and silver. For eons, this rock was eroded by the slow but consistent work of natural sculpting agents such as water, glaciers, wind, and weathering. Tiny pieces of gold eroded gradually from the exposed rock matrix through this process until they were deposited in the hundreds of miles of streambeds that dissected the numerous canyons found in the young mountain ranges.

In addition to yielding gold and silver, the mountains were responsible for other important influences on the California environment. Presenting formidable barriers to the masses of moist air moving in from the Pacific Ocean, the ranges caused the air to be uplifted to higher altitudes where it cooled and the water vapor it carried was con-

CALIFORNIA

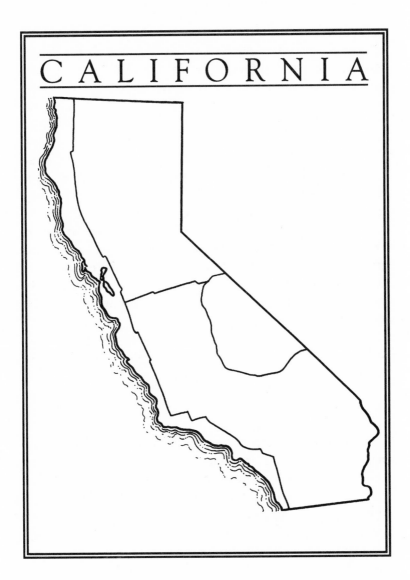

densed, eventually dropping out on the windward side as rain and snow. As a result, the western sides of the ranges received high precipitation and developed fertile soils valuable to farmers. The eastern sides, on the other hand, were denied moisture, and grew arid, eventually becoming deserts.

During the early settlement phases when people were moving into California from the east, the mountains presented formidable barriers, passage only afforded in a few selected passes. During the winter months, many of these passes were choked with snow, inhibiting movement, and countless travelers perished in the cold.

The deserts presented both advantages and disadvantages for the gold seekers who came to California. The aridity presented extreme hardships to travelers, often claiming lives. On the other hand, the exposed rock, unprotected by vegetation, weathered at a relatively rapid rate, occasionally exposing a vein of gold.

Ultimately, it was the land and its bounty that brought the people, so many different kinds of people, to this growing land of opportunity.

THE PEOPLE

Because, in part, of California's many and varied land resources, including abundant mineral wealth, most of the settlement and development of the state occurred within the past two hundred years. Initially, the early Spaniards colonized California in order to convert the natives and acquire precious metals for the Spanish treasury. Eventually, trappers, explorers, and prospectors from the midwest and east drifted into the area, found success, and returned to tell of the abundance and riches to be found in what would soon be called The Golden State. In their footsteps, a few other hardy and adventurous souls arrived. Then, in 1849, a large quantity of gold was discovered at Sutter's Mill which precipitated a flood of migration from the eastern and southern regions of the nation. Within only a few short years, tens of thousands of prospectors, miners, businessmen, speculators, and entrepreneurs traveled to California along many of the newly-opened trails to the west in search of wealth and prosperity.

And wealth was to be had. Some new arrivals became rich as a result of gold discoveries and left corporate and financial legacies that remain today. Most newcomers, however, failed in their quests to find gold. Of these, some became quickly discouraged and returned to their homes in the east, while others remained in California, eventually drifting to relatively unknown and less populated regions like Death Valley and the desert regions in the southern part of the state to try to find their El Dorado, sometimes devoting the rest of their lives to the search for gold and silver, only to have it elude them for the most part.

And then there were the few enduring and perhaps lucky, souls who, with patience and perseverance, found wealth, sometimes in impressive quantities, only to lose it. These star-crossed individuals left legacies of a different kind, legacies of lost mines and hidden treasures that have been handed down over the generations. With each retelling of the tales of gold strikes and treasure discoveries, the facts become confused, changed, and even omitted until the stories emerged as cloudy folktales and legends. But these stories, passed down over the decades like family heirlooms and old photographs, are as much a product of the people and culture of early California as anything else. Many of these stories of lost wealth remain with us today, powerful lures to contemporary dreamers who believe in the existence of the treasures—the vein of gold or silver, the long-forgotten golden ingots stacked in some secluded shaft, the hidden caches of robbery loot—in the remote corners of the state, wealth that could be discovered and possessed, fortunes that lie just beyond the horizon but always within reach of the hopeful, the dreamer.

The glory days of California's fabulous gold strikes are

long gone, the frenetic activity of that day having given way to modern commerce, industry, and tourism. But just as the early Spanish explorers, soldiers, and miners responded to the siren call of gold during the mid-1800s, a unique kind of modern-day explorer and prospector still believes in the potential of the land to yield fortunes of one kind or another. These rare and special individuals continue to comb the hills, mountains, and coastlines, to wander for days in the vast, sometimes forbidding and dangerous, deserts in search of the wealth they believe still lies hidden in some abandoned mine shaft, some remote canyon stream or long-forgotten cache.

And as with the Gold Rush of 1849, some of these contemporary argonauts find the gold or the treasure for which they search, thus fulfilling their dreams and hopes of wealth. But more of them fail, and like their historical counterparts, a portion of them return home, discouraged and disheartened, never to try again. Others of a more durable nature, the dreamers who live on hope and little else, continue to search and seek, continue to dream, fueled by the stories and the inspiration of those that have gone before them.

*　*　*

California possesses great wealth in not only mineral and other natural resources, but in folklore and legend as well. The Golden State has, over the past couple of centuries, contributed impressive quantities of colorful tradition, lore, and contemporary mythology to the nation's store of tales and legends of lost mines and buried treasures. Researching and investigating these tales can often be as exciting as the actual search for gold and silver in the mountains and deserts of the state.

In my quest to learn more about these tales and the people and places involved with them, as well as to enhance my own chances of discovery in the field, I spent many weeks in the Golden State over a period of two years. During this time I visited and explored many remote desert and mountain regions corroborating landmarks, trails, distances, and directions. I prowled the narrow canyon-like aisles of libraries, large and small, in dozens of towns. I interviewed scores of people, most of whom had memories and tales and experiences of their own pertinent to certain lost mines and buried treasures. Some of these folks have spent near-lifetimes searching for a particular cache or mine, and a few claimed to have found some of these amazing treasures.

The result of this research, as well as several months of follow-up letter writing and telephone calls, is a compilation of some of the more remarkable tales of lost mines and buried treasures associated with the state of California, many of them synthesized from various accounts and sources, most of them never-before published.

A great many tales of lost mines and hidden treasures are merely that and nothing more—stories with little or no historical documentation. With diligent research, such tales turn out to have been made up to attract tourists or fool overly enthusiastic journalists. This book only includes stories that satisfied two important criteria. First of all, they had to be good stories. Second, the tales, or at least significant portions of them, had to be verifiable through some kind of documentation. What you hold in your hands is the result of a sincere effort to capture, authenticate as much as possible, and relate some of the most compelling stories of lost gold and hidden caches from the state of California.

* * *

In California I found treasure. I found it in the abandoned mine shafts deep in the high-altitude, remote reaches of the Sierra Nevadas, the Coast Ranges, and Cascades; in many of the long-forgotten placer streams; in the waterless tracts of Death Valley, Saline Valley, and the Mojave and Colorado Deserts. In these places, I trod the same trails walked by prospectors of yore as they led their supply-laden burros and carried hopes and dreams of striking it rich in the out-crops of the mountains and canyons looming on the horizon.

While I was occasionally blessed with the luck of discov-ery, I did not come away wealthy, at least not in terms of dol-lars and cents derived from gold and silver. I did, however, come away with wealth of another sort. I discovered many heretofore little known tales of fortunes found and lost, folk-lore treasure of immeasurable value. In addition, I met and got to know many fascinating people who have spent near-lifetimes searching for some lost lode or buried treasure. I learned about their hopes and dreams, and they reminded me in many ways of the argonauts and gold seekers of the last century. I learned to understand their frustrations and appre-ciate the hardships they endured in the search for wealth. They taught me about character and determination.

In the course of researching, field-checking, and writing about California's lost mines and buried treasures, I have become intimate with some of the most fascinating land-scapes in all of North America—the majesty of the high mountains, the loneliness and challenge of the deserts, and the moods of the coastal regions, sometimes stormy, some-times serene.

I have met and traded stories and meals with kindred spirits who shared my interest in the tales, my hunger for the search, my lust for the wilderness.

I have come away with an appreciation for California, its people, its places, its history and culture. And I continue to be alternately amazed and impressed by the incredible legacy and array of folktales and legends about buried trea-sures and lost mines.

Because of what I found in California, I know I will return to explore, to search, to discover. Whether or not I find riches in the form of gold or silver, I know I will come away a wealthier man.

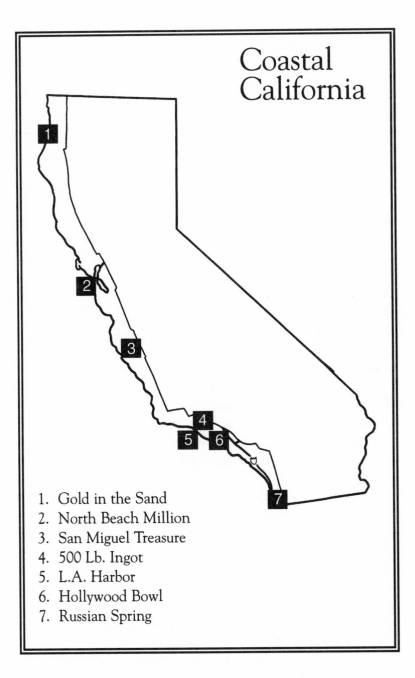

Coastal California

1. Gold in the Sand
2. North Beach Million
3. San Miguel Treasure
4. 500 Lb. Ingot
5. L.A. Harbor
6. Hollywood Bowl
7. Russian Spring

North Beach Million

THE NORTH BEACH REGION of San Francisco has always been a colorful and exciting area. During its early years of settlement, the region was regarded as a hangout for pirates and land desperadoes who frequently fought and killed one another. During more recent historic times, it has been home to numerous nightclubs, coffee houses, illegal gambling, and drug activity.

Late one evening in 1854, at some long lost location in North Beach near an old road that led from the offices of the California Lumber Company to the Broadway Wharf, a man named Harry Meiggs hurriedly buried one million dollars in gold bullion. Meiggs made several attempts to return to North Beach to retrieve his gold, but was thwarted at every turn. Today, this incredible fortune is thought to still lie beneath just a few feet of topsoil.

Harry Meiggs was a born hustler from New York City. At an early age he discovered that, with his brains and ambition, he could make money, and from the time he was old enough to realize the value of a dollar, Meiggs perpetrated one scam after another as his bank account grew to impressive figures.

Following his public school education, Meiggs was consigned as an apprentice in a lumberyard in Williamsburg, New York. This job held no appeal whatsoever for the enterprising Meiggs, but with each passing day he grew more impressed by how much money could be made providing building materials for a growing city. Over the course of the next two years, Meiggs secretly removed lumber, hardware supplies, and other goods from the yard of his employer and stocked it in a hidden location. Then one day, much to the surprise of everyone save for Meiggs, the young man opened his own lumberyard and prospered.

Eager to discover more creative ways to make money, and bored with the daily grind of operating his own business, Meiggs cast about for new opportunities. When he heard of the possibilities of making a fortune in the rapidly expanding gold fields of California, the young entrepreneur decided to travel to the Golden State. Perceiving that the booming town of San Francisco was in need of lumber for construction, Meiggs had his entire inventory loaded onto a chartered ship. He then set fire to his establishment, collected the insurance, and filed for bankruptcy. In the meantime, he purchased even more lumber and supplies on credit, added it to that already aboard ship, and a few days later calmly sailed out of the port of New York.

Meiggs was correct in his assessment of the need for building materials in San Francisco. A construction boom was taking place and the ever-enterprising Meiggs found himself right in the middle of it. It is estimated that he pocketed as much as $500,000 in profit just on the cargo he transported from New York. Meiggs decided construction was more profitable than mining gold, so he immediately undertook to have a sawmill constructed at North Beach, hired a half-dozen unemployed sailors from the docks, and proceeded to harvest redwood trees from the adjacent canyons. In no time at all, Meiggs added more laborers and was soon supplying the town of San Francisco with three million board feet of redwood lumber each month. Meiggs's new California Lumber Company was prospering nicely.

Meiggs soon became an important figure in San Francisco, both economically and socially. His fund-raising efforts led to the construction of an opera house for which he provided the lumber. Two months after he was elected to the city council, Meiggs was awarded a rich contract to build a huge pier in San Francisco Bay. Several other lucrative construction contracts came his way as a result of his political influence.

The famous Panic of 1854, the bank failure that caused thousands to go broke, created problems for Harry Meiggs. The increasing financial hardships of that period were calamitous for the businessman, but few were aware of it since he carried on as confidently as ever.

Concerned about the lasting economic depression, and burdened with loans in excess of several million dollars, Meiggs perpetrated another scam: He filed fake construction contracts with the city of San Francisco, carried them to the bank which handled such transactions for the city, and collected two million dollars in gold bullion. In response to questions posed by curious bank officials, Meiggs told them the bullion was necessary because he was involved in a sophisticated international transaction that would eventually lead to a great profit for the city of San Francisco. Temporarily placated by this answer, the bankers allowed Meiggs, with the help of several employees, to carry away the two million dollars worth of gold bars.

A city alderman, on learning of Meiggs's odd transaction, became curious and looked into the matter. On investigation he discovered that the contracts were phony, and he alerted bank officials. Meiggs soon discovered the bankers had caught onto his scheme, and he began to make hasty preparations to leave San Francisco.

Meiggs immediately chartered the barkentine, *America* which was anchored in San Francisco Bay. As he hastened to pack a few belongings, the bank officials were in communication with the local police, and soon a carriage containing three law enforcement officers and the alderman who discovered Meiggs's fraudulent scheme was on its way to the lumberman's residence. Acting on orders from his employer, Meiggs's butler greeted the lawmen, and informed them that the master of the house was on his way home, and invited the newcomers to wait in the parlor. Meanwhile, Meiggs was arriving at the offices of his California Lumber Company. There, with the help of two employees, he loaded several gold-filled canvas bags onto a waiting cab which then carried the three men and cargo into the night toward Broadway Wharf where the *America* waited, ready to sail.

Approximately midway between the lumber company and the wharf, Meiggs ordered the cab to a halt. With the help of his accomplices, he toted half of the gold bars and a shovel into the nearby woods. In fifteen minutes the men returned to the carriage, sans the gold, and commanded the driver to proceed. Around midnight, with Meiggs, his employees, and the remaining gold on board, the *America* weighed anchor and sailed into the Pacific fog.

On learning of Meiggs's trickery, the lawmen continued pursuit, even to the point of chartering a smaller sailing vessel to pursue the *America*. But it was too late.

Months later, Meiggs was reported to be in Hawaii, but by the time extradition papers arrived there, he had disappeared. Approximately a year and a half after departing San Francisco, the enterprising Meiggs showed up in South America where, in Chile, he established another lumber mill and construction company. Since Meiggs had fled San Francisco on the *America*, the police, bankers, and city officials continued to work for his extradition back to the United States. In the meantime, Meiggs commented often about his need to return to San Francisco and retrieve the million dollars he had hidden in the woods of North Beach.

Meiggs, for the moment, found greater opportunities in Peru, and moved to that country where he lived for the remainder of his life. There, Meiggs was in large part responsible for the promotion and construction of the Trans-Andean railroad. Meiggs' lumber and construction company collected over $200,000,000 for supplying all the materials for the railroad, nearly bankrupting the Peruvian government.

As the free-spending Meiggs gradually ran low on funds in Peru, he once again spoke of returning to North Beach to dig up his fortune. To that end, he applied to the United States government for amnesty from the charges still pending against him. Meiggs was so certain that his request would be granted that he began to pack and ready himself for his return. Several days later, on receiving word that his request had been denied, Meiggs suffered a heart attack. He died on September 29, 1877.

Until recently, the story of Harry Meiggs' million dollar cache on North Beach was unknown to all but a few. Since the gold was buried, the region has experienced tremendous growth: New buildings have appeared, new roads laid out and paved, and old ones abandoned.

Should anyone ever locate an 1856 map of San Francisco that showed the location of the old California Lumber Company, Broadway Wharf, and the road that connected the two, they would probably be in an excellent position to undertake a search for the lost million dollars buried by Harry Meiggs.

Gold in the Sand

FACING THE ROLLING BLUE WATERS of the Pacific Ocean along a stretch of beach just north of Arcata in the northern part of California is a weathered bluff composed of ancient rock, a mass of stone that stimulated a curious gold rush here in 1865. The man who discovered gold at this location was on his way to harvesting a fortune when he was forced out by a mining company. Growing conflict with illegal miners eventually caused the corporation to go out of business, and the mining authority was abandoned altogether. Today, the beach still contains a quantity of gold, but few are aware of its existence.

The exposed granite rock lying above the beach is grayish in color owing to the mineral content and its great age. Eons of exposure to wind, rain, freezing temperatures, and ocean storms have chiseled, sculpted, and eroded deep cuts, providing a character to the rock face much like that which deep facial wrinkles provide aged people. Portions of this bluff are extensively laced with seams of crystalline quartz— thin, shiny, sinuous seams providing further contrast to the fractured textures and pastel hues of the granite. Within the thin seams and veins of quartz, another color and texture is sometimes found—the vivid hue of almost pure gold!

Millions of years ago in this region, a huge chamber of molten magma pulsated just beneath the relatively thin crust of this portion of the North American continent. The moderate temperatures closer to the surface cooled the magma over a period of thousands of years. As the magma hardened into a great, below-ground mass of granite, some of the material near the periphery underwent conditions that resulted in the formation of gold, and it is estimated that several miles of gold-filled quartz seams are embedded in this structure today.

As a result of continual compressional stress between the North American and Pacific crustal plates, the granitic mass bearing the gold was forced to the surface at a location near the Pacific Ocean shore. Ages passed, and the constant exposure to the elements caused the rock to gradually weather and erode, providing somewhat rounded contours and a crumbly texture. As the physical bonding of the rock broke down over time from the stresses of alternate freezing and thawing, oxidation, and other weathering processes, the tiny grains fell among the accumulating beach sands which were continually deposited at the foot of the granite bluff by the ebbing and flowing of the coastal waves. As the granite wore down, so did the quartz and the gold, all of which met and mixed within the sands below.

By 1865, millions of years from the time of the original uplift and exposure of the cooled granite mass, a fortune in sediment-sized gold flakes lay just under the bare feet of those who walked the shoreline at the foot of the bluff.

During the summer of that year, a man with some small knowledge of geology was prospecting along the top of the exposed granite bluff. His name has long been lost to history, but his place in the growing accounts of California gold mining lore and legend is secure. While examining the expanse of rock, he discovered the gold-filled quartz veins and determined that ages of erosion could have deposited great quantities of the ore on the beach below. After several days spent analyzing the sands, he found the area to be incredibly rich.

For two years, the prospector sifted the beach sands, eventually extracting an impressive amount of the tiny flecks of gold. During this time, he made several attempts to file a claim on this portion of the beach, but ongoing property disputes kept him from doing so. In the meantime, he tried to organize men and capitol in order to undertake a more sophisticated mining operation. News of his discovery, however, eventually leaked out and a group of powerful and moneyed entrepreneurs stepped in to claim the riches. Time passed, and the prospector was forced to shut down his mining operation and leave the beach.

A few weeks later, an assay report was published which described the beach sands as "very rich in gold." Mining equipment was soon moved into the area and the extraction of the valuable ore from the sands commenced. The mining corporation, however, was doomed to failure from the start. Within days after mining began, severe oceanic storms ravaged the coastline for days at a time, forcing miners and engineers to abandon the beach. In addition, once the news of the discovery of gold on the beach had spread throughout the region, hundreds of prospectors and miners rushed to the area and illegally panned gold along the shore. Some of the newcomers, seeking to put the mining company out of business, sabatoged their equipment, rendering it useless for weeks at a time. Police were finally brought in and order was restored for a few days, but once law enforcement officials departed, the vandalism and renegade mining activities were renewed.

Because of these increasing difficulties as well as internal management problems, the mining company pulled out and disbanded. Fighting among the renegade miners increased, and several were driven away. Announcements of important gold strikes in the Sierra Nevada range to the east drew many more, and the severe winter storms drove the remainder from the beach. Months later, the entire beach was abandoned.

Interest in the golden sands along this part of the Pacific coast eventually waned and the fabulous discovery was soon forgotten. Well over one hundred years later, the beach lies relatively undisturbed, visited only by an occasional beachcomber or treasure hunter.

As vehicles of a variety of sizes and styles ply the paved course of Highway 101 just beyond the lip of the granite bluff, the ongoing storms and weathering processes continue to slowly eat away at the granite, gradually depositing more of the gold entrapped within on the sandy beach below.

The Lost San Miguel Treasure

THE SAN MIGUEL ARCHANGEL MISSION, located in the town of San Miguel in San Luis Obispo County, is a popular tourist destination. The mission, founded on July 25, 1797, is one of several located in this part of California. This mission has a colorful history and at one time was actually sold to an Englishman for $250. The Englishman, William Reed, was known to have buried in excess of $200,000 in gold coins on the grounds, a cache that has never been found.

The San Miguel Mission was originally founded by Father Fermin Lasuen, and during its first few years of existence consisted only of few small primitive stone and adobe thatch-roofed huts. Over a period of about ten years, this squalid cluster of hovels evolved into a small village boasting a splendid church, granary, and homes for approximately one thousand individuals, including Indians and Spanish missionaries.

As time passed, Mexico dissolved relationships with Spain, and the new independent republic did not demonstrate the same passion for maintaining the missions in California as did the Spaniards. Consequently, funding and supplies were withdrawn leaving the missions in a position to fend for themselves without outside help.

Eventually, the California missions were secularized and managed by a succession of appointed officials who knew little about such matters and cared even less. The Indians moved away and the farms, ranches, and granaries fell into disuse and decay. Soon, the San Miguel Mission was abandoned altogether.

Just a few days before the United States acquired California from Mexico in 1846, Governor Pico sold the entire mission and grounds to an Englishman named William Reed for a total of $250. Reed, an ambitious entrepreneur, converted the mission into a headquarters for the ranch he eventually established, and turned many of the outbuildings into lodging for travelers, an enterprise that proved very lucrative since the settlement was located on a well-traveled inland route between Monterey and San Luis Obispo.

Not having much faith in the durability of American currency, Reed insisted that payment for rooms and meals be made in gold, and during the first year of operation, he boasted that he had accumulated a substantial fortune from lodging travelers as well as raising cattle and fine horses.

As there were no banks in the region, Reed decided the only safe thing to do was to bury his gold coins. As he collected what many described as exorbitant rates for room and board, Reed placed the gold coins in a leather bag he suspended from his belt. When the bag became full, Reed would disappear into the adjoining yard, bury his coins at a secret location, and return within ten minutes. For approximately five years, Reed deposited his gold in this manner, and it has been estimated that he had hidden a total of nearly $200,000.

One December afternoon five suspicious-looking travelers rode up to Reed's headquarters and requested a room. The newcomers were clearly unused to horseback riding and continually cast furtive glances behind them as though expecting pursuit. During the evening meal, Reed joined the guests and engaged them in conversation. To his delight, he discovered they were also English. Happy to be among fellow countrymen, Reed ordered wine for the table and soon, their tongues loosened by the alcohol, the five men admitted they were British seamen who, weeks earlier, deserted their ship at the port in Monterey, stole five horses, and fled down the San Luis Obispo highway. Reed was concerned that the men might have been followed by law enforcement officials, and when he voiced this thought, the five strangers grew noticeably more nervous.

As one of the men went to check on the horses, another noticed the heavy leather bag attached to Reed's belt and saw that it was filled with gold coins. When he inquired about the coins, Reed bragged about burying thousands of dollars worth in a secret location behind the headquarters.

Instantly, one of the men pulled a long dagger from beneath his coat, held it against Reed's throat, and demanded to know exactly where the coins were buried. In response, Reed cursed the man who, now angered, plunged the dagger deep into the rancher's throat, killing him instantly. As two of the Englishmen rounded up Reed's wife, his two children, and the servants, the others hurried out behind the headquarters in search of a likely location in which to find the buried coins. Several holes had been dug when one of the men, growing frustrated, decided to interrogate the family.

Because Reed's wife and children had no knowledge of the location of the buried coin cache, they could provide no useful information. The men, growing angrier with each passing minute, killed all three. The servants were questioned each in turn, and when they professed ignorance of the gold, were likewise killed. In all, thirteen people fell victim to the enraged killers.

The men finally returned to the grounds and continued digging when one who had been watching the horses announced the arrival of a group of travelers. Fearing this might be pursuit as a result of the stolen horses, the men quickly mounted and disappeared into the night, riding in a southerly direction.

Following the grisly discovery of the slaughter that took place at Reed's ranch headquarters, an angry group of citizens set out in pursuit of the murderers. Several days later, the posse encountered the fleeing men just south of San Luis Obispo. Two of the Englishmen were killed during the ensuing gunfight, and the remaining three were taken to Santa Barbara where they were tried and hung within the week.

With no one to manage Reed's ranch, the area, including the headquarters and most of the outbuildings, fell into disrepair. Around 1859, the Catholic church reacquired the old mission and began restoring it. Today, the San Miguel Archangel Mission is available to the public for visitation and has become a popular tourist attraction.

Just behind the old church, a mass grave contains eleven of the victims of the slaughter that occurred over a century earlier. Somewhere close by, lying not far below the surface of the church grounds, lies William Reed's cache of gold coins, still undiscovered after all this time.

Five Hundred Pound Silver Ingot

DURING THE 1870S, SEVERAL ROADS leading into and out of the southern California city of Los Angeles were constantly terrorized by the Mexican bandit Tiburcio Vasquez and his ruthless gang of outlaws. Vasquez, accompanied by selected murderers, thieves, and cutthroats, preyed on travelers and freight wagons, often leaving their robbery victims lying in the desert sand riddled with bullets or hanging from a nearby tree. One day in 1872, Vasquez, along with his band, attacked a freight wagon and absconded with two 500 pound silver ingots, one of which remains hidden to this day in the hills north of Los Angeles.

During the gold and silver mining boom of the mid-nineteenth century, William M. Stewart made a fortune during Nevada's glory days. One of his major investments was the famed Comstock Lode from which he profited nicely. Stewart, an ambitious man who possessed a flair for politics as well as mining and business, was eventually elected to the senate in Nevada.

In 1872, William Stewart visited his brother Robert in Panamint, California, and together the two joined forces to obtain and operate a rich silver mine located in the nearby mountains.

About once every six weeks, a shipment of silver bullion was sent from the mine via pack mules to Los Angeles, approximately 150 miles to the south. While other miners and shippers suffered depredations at the hands of the notorious Vasquez gang, the Stewart mining enterprise had yet to be attacked by the outlaws. One day, however, as the Stewart brothers prepared a shipment, they received word that Vasquez waited along the trail to hold up the pack train.

William Stewart decided to wait for several days before sending out the pack train in the hope the bandit would grow weary of waiting and depart. Three days later, Stewart learned that because the pack train was not forthcoming, Vasquez had decided to conduct a raid on the mine itself. This information concerned Stewart, for while Vasquez would no doubt be accompanied by nearly a dozen fearless bandits, only about six unarmed Chinese laborers were available to defend the mine.

Stewart, normally a calm man, became frustrated at this turn of events, for following the delivery of this particular shipment of silver, he had intended to offer the mine for sale to a group of Los Angeles investors. If the potential buyers learned of outlaw hostilities in the area they would likely back off from the purchase. Finally, Stewart contrived an idea he believed might discourage the bandits.

Stewart had approximately 1,000 pounds of silver bullion packed and ready for shipment. The bullion consisted of dozens of small ingots which were to be distributed onto four mules. Stewart ordered the silver to be brought to the furnace room where he arranged for his employees to construct a large ingot mold, melt the smaller ingots, and fashion two large ones in the new mold. Each of the two new ingots weighed approximately 500 pounds, and Stewart believed the greater weight and subsequent difficulty of handling would discourage the bandits from escaping with them.

The next day, Stewart's informant told him that the Mexican bandits planned to raid the mine headquarters on the following morning, load all of the silver they could carry onto two pack mules, and flee to San Francisco where they could sell it at a good price.

On the morning of the anticipated raid, Stewart left the

ingots in the building where they were formed and, taking a pair of binoculars, retreated up the slope of a nearby hill where he concealed himself behind some brush and waited for the bandits to arrive.

About two hours past sunrise, two men on horseback rode up to the headquarters, each leading a mule. Peering through his binoculars, Stewart recognized the newcomers as two men he had beaten at cards several weeks earlier and who were known to be associated with the Vasquez gang from time to time. Finding no one at the mine headquarters, the two men casually explored around the buildings until they discovered the large ingots. Amid loud cursing at their misfortune, the newcomers wandered about the premises, gradually acquiring materials from which they constructed a crude tripod with a pulley and sling. With great difficulty they dragged one of the ingots from the building to the sling and eventually secured it. As they raised the heavy object from the ground, one leg of the tripod snapped and the entire structure toppled over.

Another half hour of labor resulted in a new tripod which, on the second raising of the heavy ingot, broke and crumpled to the ground.

On the third attempt, the ingot was finally raised and one of the mules was led under it. While attempting to lower the ingot into a crate the bandits had strapped to the mule's back, the rope broke. The heavy weight of the falling ingot struck the mule. The startled animal bolted and fled up the hillside, passing within just a few feet of Stewart.

By mid-afternoon as Stewart was tiring of watching the clumsy attempts of the would-be robbers, the two men simply gave up and rode away from the mine, leaving the two ingots lying on the ground. Stewart returned to the headquarters from his hiding place and, convinced the Vasquez would not make another attempt at raiding the mine, made preparations to transport the ingots to Los Angeles the following day.

Stewart contacted Remi Nadeau, a successful freighter who possessed a fleet of wagons as well as a stock of splendid draft animals. He selected Nadeau to transport the heavy ingots for two reasons: First of all, Nadeau had a reputation for running an efficient freight-hauling operation, generally employing several well-armed guards for important shipments; secondly, the bandit Vasquez was never known to have robbed a Nadeau shipment. Stewart never knew the reason for this, but several years earlier Nadeau, while hauling freight one day, came upon a wounded and nearly dead Vasquez about an hour after the outlaw unsuccessfully attempted to rob a train. Vasquez had been shot several times and was bleeding badly. Nadeau loaded the semi-conscious bandit into his wagon and took him to his freight station where he nursed him back to health. Since that time, a Nadeau-owned freight wagon had never been molested by Vasquez. At least not until the day Stewart shipped his large silver ingots.

After the two silver ingots were loaded into the back of a sturdy buckboard, the driver, a man named James Funk, accompanied by four armed guards, hauled them to the town of Panamint where they were transferred to a larger wagon carrying other freight bound for Los Angeles. About an hour later, the wagon, driven by Funk, departed for Los Angeles.

Approaching the city from the north, the freight wagon wound its way along the twisting trail that snakes through an area now called the Vasquez Hills. This region was characterized by hundreds of huge granite boulders spread out across more than a thousand acres. Several of these boulders were in excess of two hundred feet tall, were highly weathered, and contained thousands of shallow pits eroded out of parts of this igneous intrusive mass during the last several million years of exposure to the elements. Many of these pits were up to three to four feet deep and some of them contained water.

Approximately halfway through the maze of jumbled boulders the wagon was attacked. The guards, taken completely by surprise, surrendered immediately to the fierce-looking band. While Funk and the guards were held at gunpoint, Vasquez himself drove a buckboard from behind one of the large rocks straight toward the wagon. With the help of two of the outlaws, he slid one of the silver ingots onto the buckboard, leaving the other on the wagon.

The bandits detained Funk and the guards while the buckboard raced away to some unknown destination in the hills. Only twenty minutes later the outlaws sent the shippers on their way, telling them not to stop until they reached Los Angeles.

Immediately on arriving at the city, Funk reported the robbery to the sheriff, and within minutes a posse, intent on apprehending the bandits and retrieving the ingot, was riding toward the Vasquez Hills. Arriving early the following day, the lawmen found Vasquez's buckboard within two hundred yards from the site of the robbery, but the stolen bar of silver was nowhere to be seen.

Approximately a month later, Vasquez and his gang struck again. The outlaw directed the extortion of 800 dollars from an elderly man named Repetto who owned a large ranch located just beyond the Los Angeles city limits. As soon as Vasquez left the Repetto Ranch, the sheriff was alerted and a posse gave chase once again. The lawmen eventually caught up with the bandits near what is now Hollywood. Following a brief shootout, Vasquez, suffering several wounds, was captured and taken to San Jose where he was charged with a number of offenses. A brief trial found Vasquez guilty of the murder of two passengers during a previous stagecoach holdup and sentenced the notorious outlaw to be hanged.

Several days later, Nadeau arrived at the San Jose jail to visit Vasquez. When he asked the Mexican why, after all the years of leaving the Nadeau freight wagons alone, he decided to commit this particular robbery, Vasquez told Nadeau that he needed money badly, but reminded him that he only took one of the ingots.

When Nadeau asked Vasquez what he did with the other ingot, the bandit replied that he dropped it into one of the holes found in the rocks not far from where he took it from the freight wagon. A few days later Vasquez was hanged.

At different times, both Nadeau and Stewart searched the Vasquez Hills for the 500 pound silver ingot, but never found it. Both men were surprised to discover that there were hundreds of holes such as that described by the bandit.

To this day, the silver ingot has never been found. Many of the holes have likely been filled with sediment, effectively burying the ingot, but if someone could discern the site of the freight wagon robbery, the huge bar of silver is probably in one of the holes located within two hundred yards of that point.

Lost Gold at the Bottom of Los Angeles Harbor

ON APRIL 27, 1863, THE FERRY *Ada Hancock* exploded as it transported passengers from the loading dock at the Los Angeles Harbor to the *S.S. Senator*, a coastal steamer anchored about two miles out, bound for San Francisco. Of the fifty-six persons on board, twenty-six were killed. One of the dead was a Wells Fargo agent named William Ritchie who had carried $125,000 in gold bullion transported in three metal Wells Fargo bank boxes. The gold has never been recovered and still lies somewhere at the bottom of this busy harbor.

Ritchie was employed as a messenger by Wells Fargo and had been assigned by his superiors to deliver $25,000 in gold to the San Francisco Mint. After the *Ada Hancock* blew up, officials learned that Ritchie had carried aboard an additional $100,000 in gold. A subsequent investigation revealed that the messenger had no intention of making a delivery to the mint and planned on escaping with the gold to a south Pacific island.

Weeks before boarding the *Ada Hancock*, Ritchie was often seen keeping company with a man named Louis Scheslinger. Scheslinger was also an employee of Wells Fargo and was given the responsibility of regularly delivering large shipments of gold bullion from Los Angeles to San Francisco.

Unknown to Wells Fargo officials, Scheslinger was also involved in several crooked moneylending schemes. He would loan money at extremely high interest rates to landowners who had difficulty borrowing from a bank. Invariably, the landowner could not make the payment and Scheslinger would immediately foreclose and then sell the property for a huge profit.

During the summer of 1862, Scheslinger lent $30,000 to a Mexican rancher named Ricardo Vejar. On April 20, 1863, Vejar was killed as a result of a fall from a horse. Believing the debt would not be paid, Scheslinger drafted a foreclosure document and, accompanied by two other men, rode to the Vejar property the following day to take possession.

At the ranch, Scheslinger was met by Vejar's oldest son, Ramon, who, on learning of the reason for the visit, angrily ordered Scheslinger off the property. As the three men rode away, they were ambushed as they passed through a narrow canyon near the western boundary of the ranch. One of Scheslinger's comrades was killed and the other severely wounded. Scheslinger escaped unharmed.

Unnerved and frightened following his recent experience, Scheslinger decided to sell off his remaining mortgages and get out of the money-lending business. He managed to unload all of his mortgages to a man named Clark who paid him $100,000 with a draft on a Wells Fargo account. In the meantime, Scheslinger learned that Ramon Vejar was looking for him and intended to kill him, so he immediately made plans to leave the area. On the morning of April 27, Scheslinger appeared at the Wells Fargo office and withdrew $100,000 in gold. Frantic, he then sought out his friend Ritchie, who at that moment was preparing to leave for the harbor. The two men finally met in the lobby of the Bella Union Hotel in downtown Los Angeles where Scheslinger informed Ritchie of his plans to live someplace in the east for awhile. He asked his friend to deliver the $100,000 in gold to San Francisco for him and deposit it in a special account. Sometime within the year, Scheslinger explained, he would return to San Francisco and retrieve the gold. Ritchie agreed, and Scheslinger handed over the $100,000.

The *S.S. Senator* was anchored some distance from the shore near Dead Man's Island because its draft was too deep to enter the shallower Los Angeles Harbor. As the evening graded into night, the lights from the steamer could easily be seen from the harbor, and Ritchie regarded the huge vessel in the distance as he arrived at the Banning Dock where the *Ada Hancock* was being loaded with passengers and freight. Moments after Ritchie arrived at the harbor, Scheslinger learned from a mutual friend that the messenger had no intention of remaining in San Francisco long enough to make a deposit. According to an informant, Ritchie, immediately after debarking from the *S.S. Senator*, planned to board a steamer bound for some destination in the South Pacific. Scheslinger borrowed a pistol and set out after Ritchie.

Meanwhile, with the help of two crewman, Ritchie was loading his baggage and the three boxes of gold aboard *Ada Hancock*. After the gold had been deposited in the steamer's iron safe, Ritchie settled onto a deck chair to enjoy the cool evening air as the steamer prepared to cast off. At this precise moment, Scheslinger arrived at the dock demanding to be allowed on board. As it was not uncommon for passengers to purchase their tickets once aboard the craft, a crewman lowered a ladder and helped the newcomer climb to the deck.

Furiously, Scheslinger ran along the deck, pistol in hand, searching for Ritchie. Ritchie spotted the armed and angry Scheslinger approaching, and fled into the interior of the craft, his pursuer right behind him. As the *Ada Hancock* moved slowly across the harbor toward the waiting *S.S. Senator*, Ritchie sought safety in the engine room. Several witnesses claimed they saw the frightened man run below deck with Scheslinger in pursuit. Seconds later, several shots were heard, and then a tremendous explosion lit up the night sky, an explosion that ripped the *Ada Hancock* apart and sent it to the bottom of the harbor.

Some say the boiler exploded, others claim that a shipment of gunpowder bound for San Francisco was ignited.

Whatever the case, it spelled the end for the little ferry steamer.

Three days later, the body of William Ritchie was found washed up on shore. Scheslinger's body was not found until 1912. During the summer of that year, workers were excavating near the shoreline in preparation for the construction of a building when they uncovered a skeleton. The only clue to the identity of the remains was a silver belt buckle containing the initials "L.S."

The gold was never found. The hulk of the *Ada Hancock* still lies at the bottom of the old Los Angeles Harbor, and the three metal bank boxes containing a total of $125,000 in gold at 1863 exchange rates are still locked up in the ship's old safe, a safe that was never recovered.

The Hollywood Bowl Treasure

MOST LOS ANGELES RESIDENTS would be surprised to learn that beneath the famous Hollywood Bowl lies a huge fortune consisting of gold coins, gold and silver jewelry, and vases containing diamonds, pearls, rubies, and emeralds. This fabulous treasure was buried by a lone sheepherder who unearthed it hundreds of miles to the north and was attempting to transport it to Mexico when he was forced to rebury it. Shortly afterward, he died, and the secret to the location of the fortune passed with him.

It was a cold and drizzly autumn night when the three men, leading a pack train consisting of four heavily loaded mules, halted near the side of a low hill. The year was 1866 and the three riders, former aides to Mexican Emperor Maximilian, were searching for a suitable location to bury a fortune in gold and jewels carried on the pack animals. Months earlier, in the midst of violent political disagreement with the emperor, the three secretly removed the riches from the Mexican treasury and fled northward to where they believed they would be safe from pursuit.

The site at which they paused was located near the eastern shore of San Francisco Bay on the long, narrow San Mateo Peninsula. In later years this location was to become the heart of the city of San Bruno, but on this evening it was only remote, rocky hills and shoreline. After a few minutes of discussion muted by the sound of waves lapping the nearby shore, one of the men clumsily dismounted and walked around the immediate area as if searching for something. Presently, he pointed to a spot and called to the others who dismounted, removed some shovels from their packs, and joined the first man. In the dark they began to dig a large hole.

Clearly unaccustomed to physical labor, the three men labored for over an hour. Finally, they dropped breathless to the ground, and one of them pronounced the pit deep enough.

After the men had rested, they led the pack mules to the hole and for the next hour and a half carefully filled the excavation with two heavy wooden chests along with numerous bulky leather packs and some porcelain vases. When the last of the loads from the the mules was deposited, the pit was carefully refilled. One of the men made some notations in a small black book, and a short time later the trio disappeared into the darkness to the south. As they rode away into the fog, a lone observer, a young sheepherder, rose from his hiding pace on a nearby hill and approached the recently filled area.

After waiting for about two hours to make certain the men were not returning, the sheepherder proceeded to dig up the cache and was surprised and delighted to discover chests filled with gold coins, leather bags stuffed with gold and silver jewelry, and vases containing diamonds, pearls, rubies, and emeralds.

During the next few days, the herder secretly acquired several burros onto which he loaded the treasure, and struck out for a small village in Mexico from which he had journeyed two years earlier. His intention was to deliver this great wealth to his poor family and together they would all live in luxurious comfort for the rest of their lives.

Weeks later, as the herder guided his slow-moving pack train to the city limits of Los Angeles, he decided to cache his valuable cargo and spend a few days resting from the tiring journey. The sheepherder pulled his small caravan to a halt outside a small tavern in Cahuenga Pass. Believing it would be foolish to lead his treasure-laden burros into the bustling community, he guided them up the hill behind the tavern. Here, near a grove of trees, he dug six separate holes and filled each one with portions of the treasure, keeping some of the gold coins out for himself to spend in town. On a nearby ash tree he paused long enough to carve his initials, hobbled his burros to graze on the rich grass that grew on the hillside, and then walked into town.

For the first time in his life, the sheepherder found himself in a large city. For a long time he gazed in wonder at the hordes of well-dressed people, the wide streets, and the many buildings. He entered a restaurant and ordered a fine meal and later, filled and somewhat rested, the young man decided to go to a saloon. For the next three hours the sheepherder drank a great quantity of whiskey and eventually became violently ill. An old man named Jesus Martinez, who was employed by the tavern owner as a caretaker, noticed the condition of the sheepherder, guided him out of the establishment, and led him to his home where he provided a bed.

The next morning the young man was so sick he could hardly move. Martinez, assuming the youth was recovering from a serious hangover, served him some coffee and told him to rest. Later that day, the sheepherder suffered from a high fever and delirium. The old man soon realized the sickness was more serious than a hangover and believed the sheepherder was going to die.

During his last few moments of consciousness, the young man told Martinez about the treasure buried on the hill behind the tavern in Cahuenga Pass. Believing the youth was speaking purely from his delirium, Martinez gave little credence to the story of the fabulous cache of gold and jewels. The next morning, Martinez awoke to discover his young guest was dead.

For several weeks, Martinez, who was about seventy-seven years of age, pondered the story of the treasure cache in Cahuenga Pass. One afternoon, he related the tale to a young boy named Jose Corea, and together the two decided to investigate.

One cool, drizzly morning, Martinez and Corea rode their burros out to the pass and located the tavern. The short journey tired the old man, and he had to pause often to dismount and rest. As the two finally approached the tavern the drizzle turned into a light but steady rainfall.

Tying their burros to the tavern's hitching post, the two climbed the hill that rose gently in the short distance behind the tavern. Several times during the climb, Martinez grabbed his chest and sank to one knee. After a few minutes he was able to rise, and with shortened strides and labored breathing he resumed his climb. Corea, full of energy and anxious to reach the top of the hill and locate the treasure, always remained with his old friend and waited patiently until he was able to continue. As they neared the top, the light rain turned into a downpour.

Standing at the apex of the hill, Martinez spotted a small grove of trees just beyond the ridge, and together he and the boy headed toward it. It was difficult to spot any fresh excavations in the rain-splattered ground, and the two sought shelter from the storm in the grove of trees. As they waited for the rain to abate, they huddled under the overhanging branches of a large tree. As Martinez rested against the tree trunk, he looked about the area and discovered the initials of the sheepherder carved into a nearby ash.

As the rain continued, Martinez leaned back against the bole of the large tree and closed his eyes. Seated next to him, Jose Corea waited patiently for the shower to cease so that they could resume their search for the treasure.

About an hour later the sun broke through the clouds. Corea attempted to nudge the old man awake but he wouldn't stir. On closer investigation, the boy discovered Martinez was dead.

With the deaths of the sheepherder and his old friend, young Corea began to believe the treasure was cursed. In fear, he ran from the hill and reported the death of Martinez to the authorities. He never said anything about the buried treasure, and for the next fifteen years of his life he kept it a secret.

By 1880, numerous cattle and sheep ranches had sprung up all over southern coastal California, and travelers through Cahuenga Pass often observed hundreds of sheep grazing the adjacent hills. One morning, a sheepherder sat on a hilltop above the pass watching his flock. His attention was suddenly diverted to a nearby grove of trees where his dog was frantically digging into the ground. Curious, he walked over and discovered the animal had unearthed an old leather sack. The herder opened the sack, discovered several handfuls of coins and jewels, and gasped.

Before long, the story of the discovery spread throughout Los Angeles and Jose Corea, now a city policeman, listened with interest. According to reports, Corea learned that the herder removed treasure from only one hole, and he recalled that old Jesus Martinez once told him that six individual caches were supposed to be planted on the hill. Having long lost his fear of the curse he once imagined was associated with the treasure, and believing he might be able to locate one or more of the other caches, Corea decided to wait until the excitement about the treasure died down and attempt to search for the balance.

About six months later, Jose Corea traveled to the hill in Cahuenga Pass and climbed to the ridge where he and Martinez had spotted the grove of trees so many years earlier. But this time something was different. The small grove of trees no longer existed, and the entire area had been plowed and planted in hay.

Discouraged, Corea returned home and concerned himself with the treasure no longer. A few years later he was killed in the line of duty while attempting to arrest a felon.

In the years that followed, this part of southern California prospered and grew. Dirt roads became major highways and tall steel and concrete buildings stretched toward the sky. Thousands of acres of countryside around the ever-expanding city of Los Angeles underwent intensive development. At the small hill in Cahuenga Pass where a treasure worth millions of dollars was buried in 1866, developers have moved thousands of tons of rock and earth in order to construct the famous Hollywood Bowl which now rests on this site.

Buried Gold at
Russian Spring

BETWEEN THE SOUTHERN CALIFORNIA coastal cities of Coronado and Chula Vista is a cache of gold coins worth millions of dollars. The coins were buried by ship captain Henry Brown who feared they would be stolen by pirates. Brown was never able to return for the treasure, and subsequent erosion of the shoreline and destruction of area landmarks has rendered its location a mystery.

By the beginning of the nineteenth century, Captain Henry Brown had commanded ocean-going vessels for nearly twenty-five years and was regarded as a competent and reliable seaman. Major shipping agents who handled important cargoes of great value often sought out Brown's services for they knew they could always depend on him.

During the spring of 1802, Brown was sailing his vessel, the *Determined*, northward along the west coast of Baja California. Months earlier, the captain had sailed out of Boston harbor with the ship's hold filled with trade goods bound for the growing settlements along the California coast. Among the goods he carried was approximately $60,000 in gold coin tightly packed in a metal box and bound for an investor in San Francisco.

After rounding Cape Horn at the southern tip of South America, Brown learned that the Pacific waters were rife with pirate ships, most of them flying Spanish flags and commanded by shrewd and desperate men who discovered that the taking of unarmed merchant vessels was an easy way to acquire fortunes. Nervous about being attacked by one of these outlaw ships, Brown doubled the watch and remained constantly on guard.

Weeks later, as Brown plied a course northward, parallel to the Baja shore, one of the *Determined*'s watchmen caught sight of a sail on the western horizon. Using his telescope, Brown determined that the newcomer was on a course that would soon intersect his own. Fearful that the unidentified ship might be manned by pirates, Brown ordered the gold brought up from the hold and readied for transport to shore.

While the oncoming ship was still several miles away, Brown ordered the gold loaded into a rowboat and, accompanied by a half-dozen crew members, transported it to the nearby shore. Brown piloted the small craft to a point along the coast located just downslope from Russian Spring, a well-known source of fresh water where men who sailed this part of the ocean routinely stopped to refill their water kegs. Not far from the spring, Brown supervised the excavation of a deep pit into which he placed the gold-filled metal container.

Moments later, Brown and his crew returned to the ship, secured the rowboat, and continued northward. As the worried captain watched the distant approach of the unidentified vessel, he made an entry into his logbook about the caching of the gold, and on a separate piece of parchment he sketched a map showing the location of the buried treasure.

By the time Brown passed the port of San Diego a few miles to the north, the oncoming vessel was close enough to be identified, and the captain was relieved to discover it was not a pirate ship at all, but rather a merchant vessel much like his own. Because he was committed to a rather tight schedule, Brown continued northward with the intention of retrieving the buried gold on his return trip.

Once in San Francisco, however, Brown fell ill and was confined to bed for several weeks. As he fought a high fever, his ship remained docked in the harbor where it was being loaded with freight for the return trip to Boston.

During Brown's third week of sickness, the *Determined* was stolen from the harbor and sailed out to sea. The ship was never seen again and it was believed the cargo was removed from the hold and the vessel scuttled several miles off the California coast.

Discouraged by the loss of his ship and weakened by his lingering sickness, Brown lapsed into a severe depression and was eventually sent back to Boston. The venerable sea captain was never to board another ship; he died in his sleep two years later. The matter of the buried gold near Russian Spring was forgotten until a strange occurrence brought the incident to light nearly fifty years later.

One morning in the summer of 1847, Brown's granddaughter received a curious message from an antique dealer in San Diego. The dealer had somehow come into possession of Captain Henry Brown's sea chest, a large carved and inlaid wooden trunk that was last seen aboard the *Determined*. The chest, according to the dealer, was filled with papers, charts, and maps. The granddaughter, in the company of her brother, traveled to San Diego to examine the old trunk.

While poring over the contents of Brown's sea chest, the two descendants discovered the entry in their grandfather's logbook pertaining to the buried gold near Russian Spring. A few moments later they discovered the map that apparently showed the precise location of the fortune, only a few miles down the coast from their present location. Determined to travel to Russian Spring and retrieve the gold, the two made plans to leave for the area the next morning.

When Brown's grandchildren arrived at the prescribed area the following day, they were surprised and dismayed to discover that the shoreline and other features recorded on the map and in the logbook did not in any way resemble the current geography. During the years that had passed since the gold was buried, ocean storms had buffeted the coast, eroding tons of shoreline in places and depositing the sandy debris elsewhere. Brown's map and descriptions were useless!

Despite this immediate setback, the two continued to believe they could find the gold once they located the old spring. This too proved difficult, for the original spring had long since dried up and fresh water gushed from at least three other sources in the immediate area.

Discouraged, the grandson returned to Boston, but the granddaughter decided to remain in San Diego and continue to look for the gold. Her attempts were in vain, however, and she finally departed.

Today the area around the old Russian Spring has changed dramatically since Captain Henry Brown buried the gold coins. Immediately north of the alleged treasure site is the growing southern California town of Coronado, and just to the south is Chula Vista. Virtually every mile of beach has been developed, commercialized, and modified in some way. But somewhere near the long forgotten site of Russian Spring and several feet below the surface lies an incredible fortune in buried gold—gold that has remained hidden for nearly two centuries and is worth millions of dollars today.

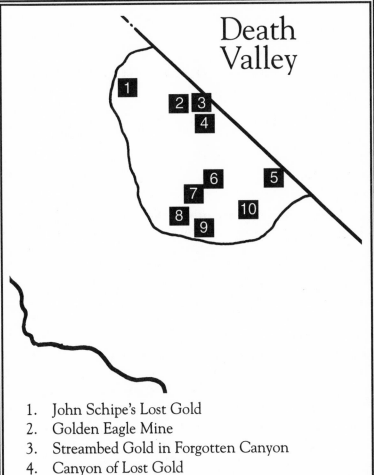

Death Valley

1. John Schipe's Lost Gold
2. Golden Eagle Mine
3. Streambed Gold in Forgotten Canyon
4. Canyon of Lost Gold
5. Breyfogles' Gold
6. Garbage Dump Mine
7. Blue Ledge of Gold
8. Goler Wash
9. Argus
10. Curse of the Mormon's Silver Ledge

The Lost Golden Eagle Lode

In the early days of this century, a crusty old desert-wise prospector known only as Alkali Jones discovered what many believe to be one of the largest deposits of gold in North America—a huge exposed quartz vein located somewhere in Death Valley, a vein densely matted with almost pure gold. Whether Jones ever successfully mined any of this gold is open to question, for he disappeared one day while returning to the lode. Since that time, over ninety years ago, the fabulous gold strike has never been relocated.

Perhaps his name wasn't actually Alkali Jones, but that was what he preferred to be called and how he was known to many in and around the mountains and deserts of southeastern California. After about twenty-five years of unsuccessfully searching for a major strike in the region of Death Valley and the Panamint Range, Jones decided to pack his burro and leave the small settlement of Skiddoo where he lived and travel to Searchlight, Nevada, where some impressive strikes had recently been found. A few days later, after traveling along the eastern flanks of the Panamint Range, Jones turned eastward and struck out across Death Valley, a relatively flat, arid wasteland that had claimed the lives of many a prospector and miner over the years.

Though he carried just a bit less than a full gallon of water, Jones was confident he would be able to make it to a well-known spring in the Armagosa range several miles to the east before running out. Temperatures in the valley soared to 115 degrees, and he and his burro quickly con-

52

sumed the little water he carried.

On the morning of the third day, while crossing Death Valley, a blinding sandstorm struck the area, reducing visibility until Jones could barely see three feet ahead of him. Holding tightly to the reins, he pulled the burro forward into the swirling sands while searching for shelter. Finally, Jones came to a jumble of large granite rocks, into the midst of which he led his pack animal. Here the two waited for several hours until the storm abated.

When the winds grew calmer, Jones left the shelter of the rocks and climbed a low, flat-topped hill to get his bearings. As he approached the hill, he had to cross several low sand drifts recently deposited by the storm. While scrambling up the north side of the highly weathered granite elevation, he spotted a glistening vein of bright quartz. Out of habit, Jones pulled his small pick from his belt and broke off a piece to examine, and he was startled to discover it was thickly laced with the purest gold he had ever seen. Each place he hammered at the bright quartz yielded gold, and the vein, over three feet thick, snaked up the side of the huge outcrop for over a hundred yards. Here, thought Jones, was truly the richest deposit of gold ore in the world, a fortune fit for a kingdom.

Over the next two hours, Jones chipped enough gold from the quartz to fill his canvas ore bag—about ten pounds worth. Tiring from the effort in the stifling heat of the day, he finally sat down to rest. As he longed for a cool drink of water, a shadow crossed the ground just in front of him and, as he looked up, he spotted a golden eagle flying low over the hill. Believing the bird was an omen, Jones christened his discovery the Golden Eagle Mine. After returning to his burro, he wrote a brief description of the lode and placed it in a used tobacco can which he buried under a mound of stones. This would serve as a claim to the outcrop until such time as he could file a formal one.

Though enthralled with his marvelous discovery, Jones

was painfully aware of his need for water. If he was to live to enjoy the fruits of his labor at the Golden Eagle Mine, he needed to find some immediately.

After leaving the site of the gold-filled quartz vein, Jones continued his journey until he came to Coffin Mountain, a prominence located in a relatively small range called the Black Mountains. Here he stopped to rest himself and his burro and sketch a map of the location of his gold. The map was crude, but showed locations of important landmarks and provided distances and directions.

When Jones completed his map, he noticed a flock of doves flying into a nearby canyon. To those who have spent time in the desert, the appearance of a dove is always encouraging, for where these birds congregate, water is never far away. Leading his burro up the canyon, Jones found a natural basin in the granite bedrock filled with cool, clear water. At this location, the weary prospector camped for three days, drinking his fill and making plans for the fortune he expected to reap from his new-found gold.

Several days later, Jones arrived in Searchlight where he dropped some his gold off at the assayer's office. Later that afternoon, he was informed that his find was worth over $41,000 per ton, a tremendous value for that time. Impressed with the richness of his discovery, Jones took the remainder of his samples, chipped the gold from the quartz matrix, converted it to cash—approximately three thousand dollars—and purchased three extra burros from a man named Win Sherman. At the Searchlight Mercantile, he bought several months' worth of supplies.

While he was in Searchlight, Jones took his meals at Jack Wheatley's tavern where he freely discussed his discovery and showed his map to curious listeners. One day, after writing a letter to his sister in Pennsylvania and informing her of his find, Jones loaded his burros and set out to return to his Golden Eagle Mine.

All along the return route to Death Valley, Jones

encountered travelers, among them a few old friends. Sometimes he would remain in camp with them, often discussing his discovery, other times he professed a need to be on his way to the mine. Alkali Jones was last seen passing through the tiny settlement of Goodsprings on his way to Death Valley.

Several years passed by and nothing more was heard about Alkali Jones and his rich mine. Most who knew the old-timer simply presumed he dug a fortune from the ground and retired to some quiet coastal town. Others believed the old prospector had been followed into the desert and murdered by men who wished to learn the location of his rich strike. Still others believed he was the victim of a rattlesnake bite, heat stroke, or a heart attack. By 1912, most people had forgotten about the old man and the Golden Eagle Mine, but one day interest in Alkali Jones was rekindled because of a visit by two Shoshone Indians to the town of Panamint Springs. The Indians had found an old pack far out in the middle of Death Valley and brought it to the storekeeper. After examining the contents of the pack, it was discovered it had belonged to Alkali Jones! Several days later, the Shoshones led several men to the site where the pack was found. Though the area was searched for a day and a half for some clue pertinent to Jones or his mine, they found nothing.

A year later, while exploring the area near where Jones's pack was found, a young prospector discovered a pile of human bones. It could never be determined if the bones belonged to Jones, nor could the cause of death be ascertained.

During the course of the next few years, interest in Alkali Jones's Golden Eagle Mine increased to the point where several prospecting parties entered Death Valley attempting to locate it. Intense heat, aridity, and the remote, rugged desert caused many of the searchers to abandon the quest early, but those hardy souls who endured were surprised by some unexpected difficulties. For one thing, Jones's geography, at least as it was recalled by those who had seen his map, was imprecise, and there was great confusion about the locations of several pertinent landmarks. For another, one investigator concluded that the constantly drifting sands had probably covered up the low hill which contained the gold-filled quartz vein.

In 1945, a geologist named Simmons learned of the lost Golden Eagle Mine and was determined to search for it. After studying all the information he could locate about Alkali Jones and his elusive gold, Simmons entered Death Valley and proceeded to a region he believed might contain the rich vein. After spending several days in the area, he chanced upon a low mound of rocks located near a jumble of granite boulders and, on investigating, discovered a rusted tobacco can buried deep within containing a hand-written note. Though the writing had long ago faded from the dried out sheet of paper, Simmons had no doubt it had been penned over forty years earlier by Jones himself in the process of establishing his claim. If this was his marker, thought the geologist, then the exposed vein should be close by. As he scanned the area, however, Simmons could find little that was not covered in deep sheets and dunes of windblown sand.

Some day, the Death Valley winds may uncover the long, thick quartz vein densely laced with rich gold. Perhaps someone will be present when it occurs, perhaps not. But as the persistent and ubiquitous winds continue to shift and carry the desert sands, the vein may be quickly covered up again.

Even if someone should locate the phenomenal deposit, yet another difficulty looms: the site of Alkali Jones's Golden Eagle Mine is now located within the boundaries of the Death Valley National Monument. This multimillion dollar lode would legally come under the supervision of the federal government!

John Shipe's Lost Gold Mine

ABOUT SIXTY MILES EAST OF FRESNO, not far from the small community of Hume, there is most likely a rich deposit of gold that was accidentally discovered in 1868 by a settler named John Schipe. After carrying some of the gold ore into town to be assayed, Schipe was killed before he could return to his mine.

John Schipe was a German immigrant who tried in vain to coax a few crops from the thin soil of his Pennsylvania farm. His lack of success at farming, coupled with a strong wanderlust, caused Schipe to travel westward in search of opportunity and adventure. In 1862, he settled in a valley some twenty-five miles east of Fresno. Known for many years as Schipe's Valley, it is now called Squaw Valley. Schipe took an Indian wife and had some small success raising cattle and hogs, growing a few garden crops, and hunting and trapping. From time to time, Schipe would join parties of miners who prospected for gold and silver throughout southern California and, over the years, gained a great deal of experience.

To many, Schipe epitomized the cheerful, backslapping, fun-loving German with a keen zest for life. Others, however, perceived him as a man who possessed a mean streak. Prone to drink too much, Schipe often instigated brawls during his frequent visits to local taverns. Though it was never proven, Schipe was believed to have killed at least six men.

Schipe would leave his cabin for weeks at a time to explore and prospect for gold along the nearby South and Middle Forks of the Kings River. Occasionally he would find some small amount of placer ore which he would use to purchase whiskey on his next visit to town, but the big strike always eluded him.

One day Schipe took his twelve-year-old nephew along with him on one of his prospecting trips up the South Fork of the Kings River. For two days, the German panned the stream but found barely enough gold to justify the time invested in the enterprise. One afternoon, the nephew discovered some fresh bear tracks and Shipe, knowing he could sell the hide in Visalia, decided to hunt for the animal. For nearly two hours they tracked the bear up the valley and into Kersarge Pass as storm clouds began to thicken above the surrounding ridges. Soon, a heavy rain began to fall and the two scrambled for shelter, eventually taking cover in what appeared to be the entrance to an old mine shaft.

As the storm raged, Schipe decided to explore the tunnel. The shaft was barely over four feet high and about three feet wide. Fashioning a crude torch with some dried twigs and grasses found just inside the entrance, the German crawled into the darkness of the tunnel only to discover it was less than twenty feet long. At the end of it, however, he discovered a seam of gold reflecting back at him in the flickering light of his torch. Taking his knife, he removed several pieces of the malleable ore and stuffed it into the utility bag he kept tied to his belt.

When the storm finally abated, the bear tracks had been washed away, and Schipe and the nephew returned home. The next day, the German carried his ore samples to Visalia, about twenty-five miles to the southwest, where he had them assayed. Later that same afternoon as he was drinking whiskey in a local tavern, the assayer approached Schipe and informed him that the ore he had brought in was almost pure gold and that his discovery was worth a fortune. Slightly inebriated from the whiskey he had been drinking, as well as overwhelmed with the joy of his new-found wealth, Schipe loudly proclaimed to everyone present that he had made a tremendous gold discovery and ordered drinks for everybody.

As several patrons of the tavern quizzed Schipe on the location of his find, he initially remained cautious and close-mouthed, but after a few more drinks he told several men that it was in a small shaft located about a half mile up the South Fork of the Kings River. Presently, Schipe realized his mistake and kept to himself.

Later that same evening, Schipe looked up his old friend William Owens, the Tulare County sheriff. He told Owens of the find, showed him some of the gold, and asked him if he would like to become a partner in mining the ore. The two men shook hands in agreement, but before leaving, Owens told Schipe to refrain from drinking so much and talking about the location of the mine.

Instead of following Owens' advice, Schipe continued to wander from bar to bar consuming whiskey. At each stop, he announced his discovery and bought drinks for everyone. Around midnight, the German began to get boisterous and quarrelsome, and town marshall John W. Williams was summoned. Williams, accompanied by Deputy James McCrory, arrived at the tavern and asked Schipe to calm down or spend the next few days in jail. Too drunk to fully comprehend the marshall's request, Schipe grew even more belligerent and challenged the lawmen to a fight. When Williams asked several of Schipe's friends to get the German to calm down, Schipe charged the marshall and began beating him with his fists. Williams and McCrory attempted to subdue the drunken celebrant, but the German was too strong for the two of them. Finally, both men drew their pistols and shot him.

John Schipe, at thirty-two years of age and apparently on the verge of becoming one of the wealthiest men in California, lay dead on the barroom floor, his blood seeping out of his wounds and puddling about his body.

With Schipe's death, many who heard the story of his

gold discovery began to search the area of the South Fork of the Kings River for the mine. Most of the searchers returned from the region having found some small amount of gold in the stream, but the mysterious small shaft described by Schipe eluded them. For the next several years, the tale of the lost mine grew and spread throughout the countryside, attracting even more searchers. In 1881, a prospector named Kenawyer arrived in Visalia claiming to have discovered what was now called the Lost Schipe Mine. After gaining the interest of a few investors, Kenawyer led a return trip to the site where it was determined he had actually found copper, not gold.

In 1888, three men were eating dinner in a Fresno tavern when one of them, an Indian, revealed to his companions that he knew the location of the Lost Schipe Mine. He claimed he had been friends with Schipe for many years, was related to his widow, and had visited the mine on several occasions. The Indian said the mine was located several miles east of Sampson's Flat on the Kings River. During the meal, the two companions pleaded with the Indian to lead them to the mine, and he finally agreed.

Two days later, the three men were camped high in the mountains overlooking the South Fork of the Kings River. Following the evening meal, the Indian told the two men they would arrive at the mine around mid-morning of the next day, and with that they all retired to their bedrolls. During the night, however, the Indian was awakened by whispered conversation between his two companions. Pretending to be asleep, he overheard the two plotting to kill him once the mine was located. Just before dawn, while the two men were still sleeping, the Indian quietly gathered his belongings and slipped away, never to return to the area. Two years later, the skeletons of his two companions were found in the valley of the South Fork. Some claimed the two men got lost and starved. Others say they froze to death in a blizzard. And still others maintain they were murdered by the Indian.

About two years later, a Mexican prospector named Hilario Gomez accidentally discovered the Schipe Mine and dug out several small sacks of the gold ore from the thick vein. Returning to Mexico, he organized a party of eleven friends to return to the Kings River region to mine the gold. On arriving at the site of the shaft, the Mexicans were attacked by Indians and all were killed save for Gomez, who managed to escape in spite of several wounds. Gomez retreated to Los Angeles where he spent nearly a year recovering. Once he was able to travel, he purchased two burros and supplies and returned to the canyon of the South Fork.

On returning to the mine, Gomez discovered the skeletons of his companions scattered about. After burying them, he proceeded to mine the gold from the small shaft, ever alert to the potential presence of Indians. Throughout the winter he worked hard and gathered several thousand dollars' worth of ore. But when spring was only a few weeks away, Gomez was stricken with pneumonia. Sick, terribly weak, and unable to continue digging the ore, the Mexican decided to load what gold he had accumulated and return to civilization. As he left the mountains and traveled toward San Francisco where he hoped to have his pneumonia treated, he grew worse and was barely able to ride his burro. By the time he reached Stockton, he was delirious and raving when he rode up to a ranch house, begging for help.

A rancher named Sharpe, realizing the Mexican was near death, provided Gomez with a room and care. As his condition grew worse, Gomez called the rancher to his bedside one evening and told him about the Lost Schipe Mine. In appreciation for his care, the Mexican gave Sharpe his gold and burros as well as directions to the mine. Several days later, Gomez died in his sleep.

As soon as Sharpe could make arrangements for a neighbor to look after his ranch, he set out in search of the mine. Arriving in the canyon of the South Fork, he encountered a late season snowstorm which forced him to return to Stockton. At Stockton, Sharpe made friends with the owner of a nearby ranch and he eventually told him about his quest to find the Lost Schipe Mine. Interested, the rancher and Sharpe agreed to become partners, and as soon as the weather warmed up sufficiently, the two men, accompanied by three pack horses and several weeks' worth of supplies, departed for the canyon. On the way, Sharpe attempted to ford the San Joaquin River that was surging with flood waters. As he neared mid-stream, his horse lost its footing and panicked. Sharpe, who couldn't swim, was washed out of the saddle and downstream in the raging torrent. It was weeks later when his body was found seven miles away, washed up on a gravel bar. Sharpe died without revealing the directions to the mine.

During the next twenty years, dozens of others have searched for the Lost Schipe Mine and a few even claimed to have discovered it. None of the claims, however, held up under investigation. To this day, the small shaft located somewhere in the valley of the South Fork of the Kings River continues to elude the persistent searchers who still occasionally come to this region to find their fortune.

Streambed Gold
in Forgotten Canyon

CERRO GORDO PEAK IN INYO COUNTY rises 9,184 feet above the arid plain, overlooking Saline Valley to the north and the Cottonwood Mountains to the northeast. During the days when prospecting and mining were flourishing in this region, a well-used trail wound from the old silver mine on Cerro Gordo Peak through the Saline Valley and eastward across the northern reaches of Death Valley toward settlements in western Nevada. Somewhere in Death Valley, just a few miles south of this old trail lies a long forgotten canyon, the bottom of which may be lined with gold nuggets nested in a layer of black sand about eighteen inches below the dry, gravelly stream bed.

In the late nineteenth century, Porfirio Santavinas was a charcoal maker for the mining company that dug silver from the mountainside on Cerro Gordo Peak. His son, Crisanto, helped him for many years, but when the boy turned sixteen, his father sent him off to work with an old friend named Juan Reyna. Reyna constructed ore furnaces for many of the mines in the region and traveled about, visiting the sites, often to repair and maintain the structures. In 1882, Reyna was hired to build a new furnace at the mining camp near Lida, located just across the border in Nevada. One morning, Reyna and the young Santavinas departed on the long and arduous trail across Death Valley.

It was June, and the summer heat was full upon the

travelers as they made their way across the flat, rocky surface of the desert floor. Leading three pack mules loaded with supplies and tools, Reyna and Santavinas set up camp one evening next to a small spring in Saline Valley where they waited for their guide, Pedro Miranda, to join them. Just after sundown, Miranda rode into camp, and the three shared coffee and talk before retiring to their bedrolls.

In the morning, the three travelers continued along the trail to Lida through what many considered the most difficult stretch—across the salt water flats of the valley and then northeast to the rocky slopes of the Cottonwood Mountains. At a crest in this range located not far from Ubehebe Peak, the trail divided near a small spring. As Reyna started to fill his canteen at the spring, Miranda stopped him, saying the water was bad, and told him he would take them to a place where they would be able to find good water.

Leading the animals, Reyna and Santavinas followed the guide along a narrow trail that paralleled the top of a ridge, finally ending at the head of a large canyon. Miranda searched for several minutes before finding a place where the mules could safely descend to the bottom of the deep gorge. Once in the canyon, the men followed the dry stream bed until it veered eastward, finally entering Death Valley.

At the bend in the canyon where it turned toward the east, Miranda dug a shallow hole in the gravel, and within minutes it filled with cool, clear water. After satisfying his thirst, Reyna commented on the sweet taste of the water. After all had tasted of the fresh liquid, they agreed to camp for the night at this location.

When the three had finished dinner, Reyna returned to the shallow hole to refill his water jugs. After capping the last one, he caught a glimmer of something in the black sands at the bottom of the little pool of water. Scooping up a handful of the sand, he swirled it around in his palm. After the fine, light grains of sand had trickled from his hand onto the canyon floor with the swirling water, Reyna was amazed to discover several small gold nuggets lodged in the creases of his weathered palm. Placing the nuggets in a shirt pocket, he scooped up several more handfuls of the dark sand, each with the same result.

Calling his friends over, Reyna showed them the gold. The three imagined that the entire canyon floor beneath the layer of stream gravel held similar gold-filled black sands, and they made plans to return to the canyon someday to mine it.

The next morning the group continued down to the mouth of the canyon and out into Death Valley. After traveling about a mile, they looked back toward the canyon and were collectively surprised to discover the entrance could not be seen. The extremely narrow opening and the high, vertical walls made it appear disappear against the irregular face of the mountainside. The three men continued on, eventually rejoining the Lida trail.

Crisanto and Reyna finally arrived at Lida, completed the new furnace in a few weeks, and then moved on to another job elsewhere. Several months passed, and the two finally returned to Cerro Gordo. When Crisanto told his father about the gold they had discovered in the remote canyon and how he intended to return for it, the old man scolded him for being foolish and reminded the youth of the hostile Indians in the area. Out of respect for his father, Crisanto refrained from immediately going back to the canyon and bided his time, intending to return at the first opportunity.

More time passed, Porfirio Santavinas passed away, and Crisanto married and moved to the small town of Isabella where he found regular employment in order to support his wife and growing family. Because of his new responsibilities, Crisanto found it increasingly difficult to return to the gold-filled canyon in the Cottonwood Mountains. He often thought of the bright gold he had seen in the black sands under the stream gravel and, in his dreams, he continued to make plans to relocate and mine the gold.

One day in 1904, two men from Illinois arrived in Isabella requesting an audience with Crisanto. They told him they were friends of Juan Reyna who had told them about the secret of the gold-filled stream bed in the faraway canyon, and asked Crisanto to lead them to the site for a share of the profits. Crisanto was unable to leave his job and family, but struck a deal with the two men wherein he would provide directions to the canyon in return for a portion of the gold. After sketching a map and providing directions, Crisanto bid the two men good luck as they led their supplies-laden mules along the trail that bisected Saline Valley and snaked its way toward the Cottonwood Mountains.

The two men, unaccustomed to desert travel, had a difficult time following Crisanto's map. After straying from the sometimes dim path several times and running dangerously low on water, they finally reached the spring near Ubehebe Peak where the trail divided. Unclear on which fork to take, each man selected a different direction, agreeing to meet back at the spring in a week.

Exactly one week later, the man who took the north fork of the trail returned, but his partner was nowhere to be seen. For two days he camped at the crossing and, finally growing concerned over the fate of his friend, returned to the settlement at Cerro Gordo Peak and enlisted some men to help conduct a search for the missing man.

Several days later, the partner was found in Saline Valley, about a mile south of the old trail. He had apparently exhausted his water supply, became lost, and after wandering about the waterless desert, finally died from thirst. In a canvas pouch tied to his belt, the searchers found about $10,000 worth of gold nuggets mixed with black sand.

Realizing his friend had discovered the location of the golden sands, the remaining prospector tried to retrace his path in search of the elusive canyon, but after spending nearly three years exploring the Cottonwood Mountains and the surrounding desert, he found nothing and eventually returned to his home in the east.

Crisanto Santavinas continued to dream of returning to the Cottonwood Mountains to retrieve the gold, but age and infirmity kept him from doing so. Eventually, he contented himself with the wealth and happiness he associated with his family and gave up his intentions of ever finding the lost canyon.

As an old man in the late 1940s, Crisanto Santavinas told the story of the lost canyon of gold to a newspaper reporter. When the story appeared a few days later, it was picked up by the wire services and distributed to dozens of other papers throughout California and the Rocky Mountain west. As a result, hundreds of people, each with visions of great wealth, traveled to Cottonwood Mountains to try to find the golden sands. Two searchers died from accidents and several more became lost, but no one ever found the gold. As time passed, interest in the elusive canyon of gold in the Cottonwood Mountains died down and few people today remember it. But somewhere on the eastern side of this range is the entrance to a canyon, a narrow opening with sheer walls that is very difficult to locate. Just inside the entrance and at the first bend, about eighteen inches below the surface of the dry stream gravels, lies a deposit of black sand rich with gold nuggets.

Canyon of Lost Gold

AT THE BOTTOM OF SOME FORGOTTEN CANYON in the Saline Valley lies a fortune in gold nuggets. The gold was discovered by a recluse prospector while digging into the canyon floor in search of water. Weak from hunger and thirst, the prospector died within a few days, but not before relating his discovery to a sheepherder. Though many have searched, the location of the canyon of lost gold remains a mystery.

Alex Ramie was a Frenchman born to adventure. Growing up in the rugged Alpine environments of southern France in the mid-nineteenth century, Ramie, became an adept mountain climber at a very young age, often scaling high, treacherous alpine peaks and traversing dangerous glaciers. When he was sixteen years old, Ramie enlisted in the French Foreign Legion and served for nearly twenty years. During his tenure as a legionnaire, he fought in dozens of skirmishes, was wounded several times, and was eventually promoted to captain.

As much as he enjoyed climbing mountains and conquering the vast Sahara Desert, Ramie longed for new adventures, and his quest finally took him across the Atlantic Ocean and eventually to Nevada where he threw himself into the search for gold as enthusiastically as he threw himself into battles on the African continent.

One day in 1885 near Virginia City, Ramie discovered an extremely rich outcrop of gold ore, and within a few short weeks he became a wealthy man. His fortune did not last long, however, for the opportunities for gambling and drinking in this wild frontier beckoned to the reckless and carefree Ramie. Before three months passed, he had lost his entire fortune as well as the title to his mine at the card tables.

Undaunted, Ramie scraped together what little money he had remaining, purchased a burro and some supplies, and returned to the Nevada desert country in search of another strike. Luck was with the Frenchman once again as he discovered a second rich deposit of gold. Unfortunately, Ramie learned little from his earlier experience. As he converted his gold to cash and pocketed his new-found wealth, the gaming tables, liquor, and women got the best of him once again. One week, Alex Ramie was a wealthy man with well over $100,000 in his pockets, the next he was little more than a penniless prospector, a victim of his appetites.

Ramie eventually decided Nevada was bad luck for him, so he packed his few belongings and journeyed to California. For months, the Frenchman heard stories of incredible gold strikes around the Panamint Range and Death Valley, and he was determined to find out for himself.

For several years, Ramie lived the life of a recluse, prospecting and living in the mountain ranges located near the periphery of Death Valley. The more he lived alone, the more he decided he preferred remote and empty deserts to crowded, noisy cities and the temptation of whiskey and cards. Ramie found just enough ore to purchase supplies from time to time, but the great strike he hoped for continued to elude him.

Ramie's wanderings took him to the northwestern reaches of Death Valley and into the Last Chance Range. This particular section of mountains had never received the attention of prospectors as had those farther to the south, so Ramie explored the canyons and hillsides with great anticipation, poking about exposed quartz veins, searching for the gold he sincerely believed he would discover.

After about a week in the Last Chance Range, Ramie found himself dangerously low on food and water. Though he hated to leave what he considered a promising area, he decided to travel westward into the Saline Valley where he knew he could find several fresh water springs. That evening, Ramie shared the last of his water with his burro.

Misfortune once again befell the prospector. On the evening before he was to depart, a stalking cougar spooked his burro and sent the animal fleeing far from camp. Though Ramie searched for several hours he was unable to locate the animal and struck out, waterless and afoot, toward the Saline Valley.

As the sun rose in the heavens and the desert floor heated up from the increasingly direct radiation, Ramie's thirst grew intense and his fatigued and overheated body limped and staggered through canyon after canyon, seeking a route to the Saline Valley.

Around mid-afternoon when he believed he could no longer continue, Ramie found himself in a remote canyon located somewhere between Ubehebe Peak and Dry Mountain. There he spotted a thin cluster of trees and shrubs. The presence of a stand of vegetation such as this in an extremely arid environment normally suggested the presence of a spring so, with one last supreme effort, Ramie stumbled down to the site. It was dry. Through a haze of exhaustion and thirst, Ramie recalled learning from the Indians who resided in the desert that one could sometimes dig down into the stream gravels and find water at bedrock. After resting for about two hours, Ramie dropped to his knees and began to scoop a hole in the dry rocky stream bed.

After what seemed like hours, the Frenchman finally reached bedrock about three feet down. Great was his disappointment when he found no water, only a dry, crusted layer of sandstone. Disheartened, Ramie collapsed into the fresh excavation and cried at his fate. There was not even enough moisture left in his body to generate tears, and as he lay in the shallow pit convinced he would soon die, the rays from the setting sun shot reflections from numerous tiny particles in the pile of recently excavated gravel. Curious, Ramie picked out a few of them and, to his utter surprise, discovered that they were nuggets of gold!

Forgetting his thirst and exhaustion, Ramie looked about and found gold nuggets in profusion gleaming from practically every part of the stream bed, gold worth millions of dollars. He selected several of the largest and purest of the yellow stones and placed them in his pocket.

As fatigue overtook him, Ramie fell asleep in the shallow hole in the stream bed. About an hour before sunrise, he awoke and contemplated his turn of luck. Of course his new fortune would do him no good if he could not reach water soon. Somewhat refreshed by sleep, he pulled himself from the shallow pit and continued his painful journey out of the canyon and toward the Saline Valley beyond.

Ramie was confident that the sleep and rest he had received the previous night would be sufficient to sustain him in his search for water, but before noon the combined effects of dehydration and exhaustion began to claim him. Time and again he fell to his knees, cutting his trousers and flesh on the sharp-edged desert rock. The pain caused him to cry out but his throat was so parched that no sound passed his lips.

Finally, completely exhausted, Alex Ramie crumpled to the hot desert floor. In his semi-conscious state he realized he was too weak to rise and ultimately resigned himself to dying before he could retrieve his fortune in gold lying in the stream gravels in a remote canyon a few miles back in the range.

Two days later, a desperately weakened and sunburned Alex Ramie awakened to the sensation of water being poured into this mouth. As he slowly regained consciousness, the Frenchman realized he was lying in a crude brush shelter and his limbs were being bathed with cool water. As his saline-encrusted eyes adjusted to the dim interior of the little hut, he became aware that three Indian women were cleansing him and applying cool compresses to his head and body. He finally realized that the desert Indians had found him and brought him to their camp.

As Ramie hovered near death on the desert floor, a hunting party spotted him and carried him back to the village. For forty-eight hours, the prospector was cared for with a tenderness belying the primitive manner in which these desert dwellers lived in this harsh land.

For two weeks Ramie resided with the Indians until he felt sufficiently strong to undertake a journey to the town of Panamint. There he intended to obtain enough supplies to return to the canyon and harvest the gold from the stream bed. From time to time he would pull the nuggets from his pocket and examine them, thinking of the life of wealth and luxury more of the same would eventually bring.

On the morning Ramie departed the Indian camp, his new friends provided him with a full gourd of water and a small sack of food. Hours later, the Frenchman was once again hiking across the arid plains in the debilitating heat and blinding sun. By mid-afternoon, it became clear to Ramie that he was still not up to the long journey, and his steps grew more measured and halting. Eventually he sought shade beneath a projecting rock and fell asleep.

The next morning, Ramie was awakened by the unlikely sound of bleating sheep. As he looked about the plains lying before him, he spotted a small herd about a half-mile away tended by a lone herder. Overjoyed at meeting another human being in the desert, he staggered onward until he came to the herder's small camp.

Alfred Giraud, a Basque herder who had recently migrated to America, watched as the man staggered up to his small fire. When Giraud rose to greet the newcomer who was clearly exhausted and weak, Ramie pitched forward in a faint. Reacting quickly, Giraud dragged the limp form of the Frenchman into the shade of his rock shelter and forced him to drink some strong coffee.

For two days Giraud cared for the semi-delirious Ramie, feeding him a thin bean soup and coffee. On the third day, Ramie called Giraud to his pallet and told him about the gold he had discovered in abundance on the floor of a canyon located several miles to the northeast. Giraud thought the tales of wealth were but the mere ravings of a man hallucinating and mad from lack of water, but when Ramie pulled several nuggets from his pocket, the Basque stared in awe. "If the canyon bottom was filled with as much of this rich gold as the sick man claimed," thought Giraud, "then truly a fortune awaited the person who could return to it."

Ramie told Giraud he was grateful for his care and said he didn't expect to live much longer. With his breath labored and his voice rasping, he provided the sheepherder with directions to the canyon of gold. Giraud told Ramie that the gold belonged to the person who discovered it and assured him that once he regained his health he could return and excavate it. Ramie told Giraud he wanted to share the gold with him and that, together, the two could travel to the canyon, mine the nuggets, and become rich. He placed the fistful of gold nuggets into the calloused hands of the sheepherder, telling him it was a gift, and that much, much more awaited them in the rich gravels of the faraway canyon.

Giraud contemplated a life of wealth as he tended to his flock that afternoon, but when he returned to his shelter he discovered that Ramie had died.

Several months passed and occasionally Giraud found himself considering leaving his herd and searching for the canyon of gold. Ultimately, however, he decided that, though his life was a relatively poor one, it was filled with contentment and the Basque decided to remain a herder.

Over the next two decades, Giraud thought often of the canyon of gold and was sometimes tempted to search for it, but could never bring himself to leave his herd. One day, however, when he was nearly sixty years of age, he decided he was too infirm to continue herding sheep around the rocky desert plains and decided to try to find Ramie's canyon.

Giraud purchased a burro and some supplies and set out in search of the canyon of gold. Time had dimmed his memory of Ramie's directions, and the old Basque became lost repeatedly. In addition, with each passing day he began to realize that he was far too old to survive in the harsh desert so he soon abandoned the search.

As recently as the early 1920s, Indians would come out of the Saline Valley and the adjacent mountains into nearby towns where they would purchase food and clothing, paying in gold nuggets. When asked where the gold came from, the Indians always gestured toward Ubehebe Peak and tell of a canyon filled with such nuggets.

Using vague directions supplied by the old sheepherder and some Indians, several have attempted to locate the canyon of gold, but the unforgiving desert environment defeated them all before they could find it. Even today, this area remains rugged and forbidding, and is bisected only by a seldom used two lane highway. Protected by remoteness, aridity, rattlesnakes, and extremely difficult terrain, the elusive canyon of gold accidentally discovered by the Frenchman Ramie over a hundred years ago will likely remain lost for many years to come.

The Garbage Dump Mine

AL COE WAS TYPICAL OF MANY CALIFORNIA PROSPECTORS who wandered and explored the mountain and desert country of central to southern California during the latter part of the nineteenth century. With his burro, Coe roamed from town to town, taking odd jobs to earn just enough money to purchase supplies for another journey into the mountains in search of gold. One day Al Coe was shown a rich mine high in the Panamint Range, a mine that contained almost pure gold threaded throughout a thick quartz matrix, a mine that has never been discovered since.

Late one afternoon on an unseasonably warm day in the spring of 1872, Al Coe led his burro up a steep winding trail into the higher altitudes of the Panamint Range near Death Valley. The prospector was new to this part of the country and, having neither map nor directions at his disposal, became lost. As he followed the rocky path upward into the cooler environs of the mountains he passed through thin clumps of stunted trees and wound among large, dark grey granite boulders. Coe hoped to climb to a point higher up from which he might look out across the valley below in order to spot some familiar landmark.

As Coe walked along whistling a popular tune of the day, he was surprised by a bearded, dirty man who stepped from behind a rock outcrop located next to the trail. The diminutive man was at least sixty-five years of age, stocky of build yet shaky of leg, clad in oft-patched overalls, and he coughed uncontrollably as he leveled a rifle at the newcomer's mid-section. Shooting a hostile glare at Coe, the old man demanded to know why he was looking around in this part of the mountain range.

After removing his hat and apologizing for the intrusion, Coe nervously explained that he was lost and wished for nothing more than directions to the valley below. When the grizzled old man realized Coe represented no threat whatsoever, he lowered the rifle, scratched his white-whiskered chin for a moment, and invited the stranger to come up to his camp and share his dinner with him.

As they walked up the trail, the old man introduced himself to Coe and told him he had been working a small but rich gold mine nearby and couldn't afford to be careless about strangers. As the two walked up the trail in conversation, the old miner's speech was constantly punctuated by fits of coughing that emanated from deep within his chest. With every few steps he had to pause to spit up large masses of phlegm, and Coe noted that it was thick with blood.

A few minutes later, the two men walked into a rather unkempt camp. A crude shelter fashioned from thin slabs of local rock on a structure of tree limbs served as a residence for the old man, and it was apparent to Coe that the old-timer had lived at this site for a long time. While engaged in conversation, Coe looked all about the area but could find no evidence of a mine.

Presently, the old man had a low fire going and a pot of coffee bubbling next to the flame. After some small talk, Coe told his host he had been searching for a promising claim for several years, a search that brought him to the Panamints where he thought he would try his luck. The miner eyed Coe silently for a moment and informed him that he possessed the rights to dig in this part of the mountain, but told the newcomer that he had heard there may be gold-bearing outcrops a few miles to the north. After Coe said he would head in that direction in the morning, the old miner relaxed a bit and prepared a dinner of beans and biscuits.

Following the meal, the old miner showed Coe around his camp. He told him that he had been regularly taking gold from this spot since he arrived ten years earlier, and the vein of ore appeared to be limitless. After showing him a view of Death Valley which spread from the foothills to the eastern horizon, the old man took Coe to the site of a huge garbage dump piled against a nearby outcrop, a dump which contained hundreds of rusted cans, broken bottles, and other refuse. In between fits of coughing, he managed a small chuckle and told Coe he had been at this location long enough to accumulate an impressive pile of garbage.

The next morning after breakfast, Coe bid the old miner goodbye and returned down the winding trail to the valley below. As he led his burro along the rocky path, he thought about the persistent cough that afflicted the old man and deduced he must have an advanced case of tuberculosis. Coe also wondered why he saw no evidence of a mine shaft near the old man's camp.

For the next several months, Al Coe actively prospected around the numerous canyons and ridges of the Panamint Range. Now and then he would arrive at some small settlement to replenish his supplies and hang around the local taverns, listening to the other miners and prospectors, hoping to pick some leads on where to search for gold.

One evening while standing at the bar of the Silver Strike Saloon in the town of Wildrose, Coe overheard several prospectors talking about the strange old man he met high in the Panamint Range. The old miner was well known in the area settlements, and was often seen leading a mule into town with saddlebags filled with rich gold. The old man's gold was of a curious type not often seen in this area—the ore was threaded throughout the quartz matrix as though it had been embroidered by hand, a type of pattern referred to as a tapestry formation. People often asked the old man where he obtained his tapestry gold, but he would always just chuckle and go about his business.

Early the next spring, Coe returned to the old miner's camp in the Panamints for a visit. The bearded recluse saw him coming up the trail and walked down to greet him, but it was obvious the effort caused him great pain and discomfort. Amid several severe coughing spasms, the miner was helped by Coe back to his shelter. When his friend was finally laid down on the pallet, Coe covered him with an old worn blanket to help ward off the chill mountain air. It was clear that the old miner's health had grown progressively worse during the past year, and Coe expected he would not live much longer.

For the next several days, Coe prepared meals and generally cared for the old miner. When he realized the camp was low on provisions, Coe offered to walk to the nearest town and procure some supplies.

While Coe was bridling his burro and readying for departure, the old man came to him and told his guest he wanted to show him something. Aided by Coe, the old-timer walked with great difficulty down the slope toward the garbage dump. When the two men arrived at a point just above the dump, the old miner pointed to the pile of refuse and told Coe that the entrance to his rich mine was under all of the debris. He explained that over the years he extracted only small amounts of the gold at a time, just enough to go to town occasionally to pick up supplies. He also explained that just a few feet inside the narrow shaft could be found a thick, vertically oriented vein of quartz containing tapestry gold worth millions. The old man also told Coe that, should anything ever happen to him, the mine was his.

Coe, stunned at the description of the riches and at the fact that the location of the rich mine had been revealed to him, was speechless.

The next morning, Coe took his burro and walked toward the nearest settlement to purchase some supplies. Four days later as he climbed the steep trail that led into the old man's camp, Coe noticed that the miner was not there to greet him as was his custom. After removing the heavy load from the pack animal, Coe searched the area for his friend. Finally, after entering the crude rock shelter, Coe found the miner. The old man had been dead for at least two days, the advanced tubercular infection finally claiming him.

Saddened by the loss of the old man, Coe prepared a grave nearby, interred his friend, and said a short prayer over the rock-covered mound.

The next morning, Coe walked to the garbage dump and regarded the huge pile of debris. Taking a shovel he found nearby, he removed some of the garbage and in a short time uncovered the low, narrow opening to a mine shaft. Lighting a lantern, he crawled into the shaft and found the vein of gold-filled quartz. It was exactly as the old man had described it—a shiny quartz matrix embroidered with almost pure gold ore, undoubtedly worth millions of dollars as there appeared to be no limit to the rich vein.

During the next few years, Al Coe extracted gold from the mine in much the same manner as did the old miner, taking only a small amount and using it to purchase supplies. It was a way of life he wished to lead—quiet, peaceful, and far from the hustle and bustle of the crowded towns.

Coe worked the garbage dump mine for several years, going into town rarely. One trip to Death Valley Junction, he became violently ill from some unknown cause and passed out in the dirt of the main street of town. A man named Bert Topping was passing by at the time, and carried Coe to his home where he provided a bed and care for almost a week. During most of that time Coe remained delirious, but during his few lucid moments he kept referring to his rich gold mine in the Panamint Range.

One evening when Topping brought some dinner to Coe, the bed-ridden miner invited his host to sit beside him while he told an amazing story. As Topping listened, Coe revealed the existence of the rich gold mine hidden beneath the garbage dump high in the Panamaint Range. He told his host that, like the old miner, he believed he would not live much longer and wanted to share the secret location with him. As Topping listened, Coe provided directions to the mine.

Two days later, Al Coe died quietly in his sleep.

As soon as he could find the time, Topping filled a pack with provisions and set out in search of Coe's secret mine. For several weeks he wandered throughout the Panamints searching for the garbage dump, but found Coe's directions to be vague and confusing.

Years later when Topping attempted to describe the location to his son, he remembered only that to reach the mine you have to climb into the upper reaches of the Panamints from the west side of the range somewhere south of the town of Wildrose. From the crude rock shelter where the old miner had lived, one had a clear view of Death Valley to the east. About thirty yards from the camp down a low slope was a garbage dump that concealed the opening to what may be one of the richest lost gold mines in America.

Breyfogle's Gold

THE TALE OF THE LOST BREYFOGLE MINE is one of the most talked about in California. While Charles C. Breyfogle did indeed discover gold, he was never able to mine any of it. In fact, after discovering this very rich deposit of ore, Breyfogle, who was fleeing from Indians at the time, was never able to relocate it, and the mystery surrounding its location has attracted hundreds of searchers over the succeeding generations.

Charles C. Breyfogle was not the typical prospector roaming the hills of southern California during the last half of the nineteenth century. He was, in fact, a fairly successful businessman who held an elected office in the county of Los Angeles, and he was an individual constantly in search of new investment opportunities.

On a hot day in June, 1862, one such opportunity presented itself to the enterprising Breyfogle. Gold was discovered near the Toiyabe Range near Austin, Nevada, and Breyfogle decided to form a mining company, file some claims, and extract the ore. Breyfogle's aim was to amass a fortune in as short a period of time as possible. Gathering two business partners named McLeod and O'Bannion, Breyfogle purchased some mules and provisions and departed for Austin.

Rather than follow the established stagecoach road that wound northward to Sacramento and then eastward to Austin, the three men decided to cut straight across the desert northeastward from Los Angeles in the hope of saving several weeks of travel time. None of the men were prepared for the rigors of the hot, dusty, Indian infested barrens of Death Valley and the Panamint Range.

The three investors, all quite used to the soft living of the big city, encountered far more in the way of hardship than any of them expected. Lack of water was a constant problem, and their food supply was exhausted at the end of three weeks, forcing them to live on rabbits, snakes, and cactus fruit. The end of the first month of the journey found the three travelers skirting the southern end of the Panamint Range searching for a suitable place to camp for the night. Rainfall from two days earlier had gathered in several small rock depressions along the trail, and since the men were low on water, they decided to stop there. After hobbling the mules, the exhausted McLeod and O'Bannion stretched out on the rocky ground and immediately fell asleep. Breyfogle, finding the hard and uneven rocks too uncomfortable, walked about a hundred yards south of the site until he found a few square feet of smooth, soft sand on which to lay his bedroll. Pulling off his shoes, the weary Breyfogle lay down and relaxed into a deep sleep.

During the night a loud commotion awoke Breyfogle. From his two friends' camp he heard agonized screams mixed with blood-curdling yells—McLeod and O'Bannion were being attacked by Indians. Breyfogle estimated there were about twenty of the raiders and, fearful they would soon discover him, he grabbed his shoes and ran quickly into the night.

For several hours the frightened man fled in the darkness. Breyfogle had no idea where he was or which direction he traveled. He did not even stop to put on his shoes. The next morning's rising sun found him several miles east of the camp and in the arid wastes of Death Valley. Exhausted, Breyfogle stumbled into a dry arroyo and crawled into a slight recession in a cutbank carved long ago by some ephemeral stream. Relieved somewhat by the small amount of shade offered by the jutting overhang, the tired man assessed his situation while he examined his torn and bloody feet. His soles and toes were so mangled and swollen that he was unable to fit his feet into his shoes. Completely exhausted from his fear and his flight, Breyfogle reclined on the coarse gravel of the stream bed and fell asleep.

He awoke from his fitful slumber five hours later and, still unable to put his shoes on, stumbled painfully onward, heading generally in an easterly direction. The bright surface of the sands reflected the piercing rays of midday sun into his eyes, partially blinding him. Weakened by his flight and lack of food and water, Breyfogle searched through the harsh glare of the pitiless environment for some sign of moisture. Presently, he spotted a small spring gurgling a smokey-looking liquid from the ground. The water was heavily alkaline but, unable to control himself, the thirsty man gulped great quantities of it until he could hold no more. After drinking his fill, Breyfogle reclined on a bare rock intending to sleep for several hours, but within minutes he became violently ill from the foul water. For two days, he alternately drank the alkaline brew from the spring and retched it back up, but eventually his system grew used to it.

On the third day Breyfogle recovered, filled the toes of his shoes with water, and continued northeastward until around evening when he arrived at the southwestern slope of the Funeral Range. A strong, hot, dry desert wind had been blowing for most of the afternoon and Brefogle, deciding to stop here for the night, constructed a low wall of flat stones behind which he sheltered himself against the blowing sands. Here he drank the water from one shoe and fell asleep. The next morning he consumed the rest of the water and, though very weak, began ascending the range, believing succor would be found on the other side.

As the tired Breyfogle climbed the low slope, something to his right caught his eye. Nestled among the bleached grey of the rocks was a green tree! Vegetation often meant water, so he made his way toward the tree.

As he stumbled barefooted along the rocky slope toward the tree, Breyfogle noted another splash of color, this time at his feet. Stooping to pick up a glittering rock, he discovered it to be a cluster of very weathered porphyry of a reddish color profusely laced with gold! Pausing to examine the area where he stood, Breyfogle noted dozens, perhaps hundreds of similar gold-flecked chunks of this curious rock scattered at his feet. He gathered several small pieces and tied them into his bandanna which he then placed in the toe of one shoe. After he proceeded another twenty yards toward the tree, Breyfogle discovered the vein from which the gold had apparently eroded. The incredibly rich vein was about two feet thick, densely shot full of gleaming gold, and appeared to extend several dozen yards up the side of the mountain. Here indeed, thought, Breyfogle, was enough gold to make several men as wealthy as kings. He determined to return to this site after reaching civilization.

Finally arriving at the tree, Breyfogle was disappointed to discover there was no water. The tree, however, was a mesquite and numerous green pods hung from the branches. The hungry man gathered several fistfuls and consumed them while resting in the shade of the branches.

Somewhat refreshed, Breyfogle continued his trek, eventually crossed the Funeral Range, the Armagosa Desert, and finally arrived at a place called Baxter Springs. Here, Breyfogle revived himself on the clear cool water and ate the succulent pads of the various cacti he found nearby. After resting here for several days, he continued northward, bound for Austin.

Several days later a rancher named Wilson was searching for stray cattle on his Smoky Valley Ranch when he discovered the tracks of a barefooted man. Curious, he followed the prints for several miles and eventually caught up with Breyfogle. Wilson was the first human being Breyfogle had seen since fleeing the ill-fated camp in the Panamint Mountains. Wilson, for his part, could scarcely believe what he saw when he encountered Breyfogle. Amazingly, Breyfogle had survived a 250 mile journey on foot largely without food or water through some of the most arid and hostile country in North America. His clothes were little more than dirty rags and tatters that barely clung to his sun-darkened body. His hair and beard were filthy and tangled. Wilson initially thought Breyfogle, who was still carrying his shoes in his hands, was a demented Indian.

When Wilson finally realized Breyfogle was a white man, delirious and half-crazed from his ordeal in the desert, he took him home to his wife who nursed him back to health over the next few weeks. One day when Wilson was checking on the progress of his guest, Breyfogle reached into one of his shoes and withdrew a bandanna which was wrapped around some objects. Spreading the cloth open, he showed the rancher the gold. Wilson examined the ore and noted it was very rich. For the next hour, he listened to Breyfogle's tale of discovery of the rich vein and the pieces of gold-filled rock scattered all over the ground.

When Breyfogle finally recovered, Wilson took him on to Austin and left him with a friend named Jacob Gooding. Gooding was a miner, and when Breyfogle told him his story and showed him some of the gold, he offered to have it assayed. When the report showed the ore to be of great value, Gooding offered to organize an expedition and, with Breyfogle leading the way, return to the Funeral Mountains to locate the vein. Three weeks later, Gooding, Breyfogle, and six additional men led a mule train packed with water casks, mining tools, and provisions out of Austin. On arriving at the northeast slope of the range, however, the party was attacked and turned back by nearly fifty Paiute Indians.

Three months later, Breyfogle and Gooding set out once again to find the gold. This time they were accompanied by a dozen well-armed men and carried along several months' worth of gear and supplies. Instead of attempting to cross the Funeral Range, Gooding decided to skirt the southeastern end and come up through the more easily-traveled lowlands on the southwestern flank. After several days of travel, the party arrived at the alkali spring from which Breyfogle drank. Eventually they came to the low wall of rocks the fleeing man constructed to protect himself from the wind, and about three hours later found a mesquite tree. From the tree, the men fanned out generally in a northwesterly direction in search of the rich vein of ore and the gold-flecked chunks of red rock lying on the ground nearby. Encouraged, the men searched all day long but found nothing.

The next day a second mesquite tree was located nearby and this generated some confusion. Breyfogle grew uncertain as to which was the correct tree and his confidence wavered. For several more days the group of men searched the area before finally giving up. Discouraged, they returned to Austin.

During the years 1865 and 1866, Breyfogle made several more trips into the Funeral Range in search of the gold. Every time he encountered hostile Indians. On one occasion, he was shot twice and barely survived a serious leg wound that severed an artery. On another occasion, he was attacked and shot in the head by Paiutes. Lying unconscious, the Indians presumed he was dead and scalped him. Breyfogle carried the scars of the scalping for the rest of his life. Frustrated that he could not locate the vein of gold, he eventually gave up the search and returned to live with his wife near Seattle.

Others, on hearing about Breyfogle's gold, tried to find it. George Hearst, the father of publishing magnate William Randolph Hearst, learned of the elusive vein of gold in the Funeral Mountains and grew interested. After examining a piece of the ore Breyfogle carried out of the desert, Hearst financed an expedition that spent a total of eighteen months searching for it, but nothing was ever found.

Though few have ever doubted the veracity of

Breyfogle's discovery, the fact remains that it was never found. One searcher, a man who also located the alkali spring, the rock wall, and the mesquite tree, offered an explanation. Herbert "Yankee" Pierce undertook three different expeditions to the Funeral Range and spent a total of several months in search of Breyfogle's vein of gold before before chancing on an important discovery. According to Pierce, the area where Breyfogle claimed to have discovered the gold had been subjected to a landslide. A few months following Breyfogle's rescue, unseasonably heavy rains struck the Funeral Mountains. The moisture, according to Pierce, apparently loosened and lubricated some of the highly weathered rock and caused it to slide down the mountainside, completely covering the gold.

There is no doubt that Breyfogle's gold still exists right where he found it. According to the several assays conducted on the ore that Breyfogle carried into Austin, the vein from which it came must be amazingly rich and capable of supplying millions of dollars worth of the ore. Unfortunately, it is probably buried under several tons of rock.

Mysterious Blue Ledge of Gold

RADIATING OUT FROM DEATH VALLEY's Brown Mountain are several canyons, all of which carry away runoff from local rainstorms. During the first decade of this century, prospector Charlie Wilson discovered a curious blue quartz in a rock outcrop in one of the canyons, quartz that contained tiny flecks of what he thought was gold. Days after leaving some samples with an assayer, Wilson was killed before he learned the rock contained gold of impressive quality. Wilson provided no information on which of the Brown Mountain canyons contained the strange blue quartz, and the search for the location continues today.

It was a cool April morning in 1906 as Charlie Wilson led his string of six burros along the Ballarat Trail toward the town of Johannesburg. Wilson seldom had use for that many burros, but he accumulated the animals over the years, had grown fond of them, and continued to keep most of them as pets, providing names for each one. As the bewhiskered veteran of two decades of prospecting and mining hiked alongside the single file of pack animals, he talked to them in soft tones, chucking them on their way with gentle encouragement.

Wilson, who had just spent about six weeks in the Panamint Range, was returning to Johannesburg with several samples for assay. He had discovered some promising color in a rock outcrop in Surprise Canyon and felt certain the specimens of gold ore he carried back would prove to be rich enough to justify a full-scale mining project.

As Wilson imagined striking it rich, he continued along the road that would soon pass to the south of Searles Lake. A short distance to the east he could see Brown Mountain, a low prominence on the otherwise flat desert landscape. As it was growing late in the day, Wilson decided to camp next to a freshwater spring, a site he had visited many times in the past. The water hole was located between the trail and the mountain, and Wilson herded his burros toward it as the sun was sinking low in the west.

During the night, a heavy rainstorm struck the area, and when Wilson awoke the following the morning, the desert air was filled with a rich, clean, washed-out smell. Invigorated by the night's rest and the fresh air, the old miner ate a hearty breakfast and, picking up his prospector's hammer, went for a short walk up one of the small canyons in the low foothills of Brown Mountain. Shortly after entering the mouth of the canyon, Wilson observed signs of a flash flood that had recently surged through the shallow gorge, a flood no doubt spawned by the rains of the previous night. Here and there Wilson spied brush and debris that had washed down from higher altitudes. He also spotted several freshly eroded banks along the canyon walls. It was at one such erosional scar that Wilson stopped to examine a thick ledge of newly exposed rock exhibiting a curious blue color.

Wilson had never seen blue rock like this before, so, taking his hammer, he knocked off a piece to examine. Throughout the rock, which he decided was a kind of quartz, he spied tiny flakes of what he thought must be iron pyrite. Wilson decided to take a few pieces back to Johannesburg and have it assayed along with his other specimens.

The morning after arriving at Johannesburg, Wilson carried all of his samples over to his friend, Fred Carlisle, manager of the assay office at the Red Dog Custom Mill. After depositing the specimens taken from his claim in the Panamint Range, Wilson showed Carlisle the blue quartz he had found near Brown Mountain. In some detail, Wilson described the location of the spring and the nearby canyon in which he discovered the quartz. After leaving all of the samples with Carlisle, Wilson told the assayer he needed to travel to Los Angeles on a family matter and the results could be forwarded to him there.

Two days later, Wilson caught a stage for Los Angeles. Within the week, Carlisle completed the assay on Wilson's gold samples and sent the results to the address the prospector provided. After casually looking over the pieces of blue quartz, Carlisle decided they were worthless and put them on a shelf in a storeroom.

Several months passed and nothing was heard from Wilson. One day as Carlisle was cleaning out his shed, he spotted the samples of blue quartz left by the prospector. Convinced Wilson had long since forgotten about the curious rock, Carlisle carried them, along with a bucket of trash, to the back yard where they were thrown onto a pile of waste and set afire.

Several days later, Carlisle noticed several neighborhood children playing in the ashes of the garbage dump. After chasing them away, the assayer was distracted by a partially burnt chicken bone flecked with a golden color. Curious, he examined the bone and was surprised to discover that small pieces of gold had attached to the bone. Digging through the ashes, Carlisle found several other bones, all with tiny gold flecks stuck to them. He also found some small pieces of Charley Wilson's blue quartz.

Somehow, deduced Carlisle, some gold accidentally got into the trash and, as it melted from the heat of the fire, the lime from the chicken bones acted as a reagent to fuse the ore. Taking one of the blue stones into his office, he examined it closely with a microscope and discovered the pyrite-like flecks of color were actually gold. Charley Wilson's blue quartz was, in fact, a gold-bearing rock of impressive value, and assayed at more than $15,000 to the ton!

Believing this discovery was important, Carlisle immediately sent word to Wilson in Los Angeles. Several weeks passed with no response, so Carlisle decided to travel to the coastal city, find Wilson, and tell him the good news in person.

After searching for his friend Wilson for three days, Carlisle finally went to the police station to make inquiries. Here, the assayer learned that Wilson had been killed the very day he had arrived in the city, struck by a streetcar. Saddened by his friend's death, Carlisle returned to Johannesburg.

During the following weeks, Carlisle tried vainly to remember Wilson's directions to the ledge of blue quartz, but the passage of time had dimmed his memory. Eventually, he gave up attempting to recall the location of the rock and placed the samples, along with the gold attached to the chicken bones, on a shelf.

In 1916, James Nosser came to Fred Carlisle with a request to learn assaying. Carlisle readily agreed, and the eager Nosser quickly learned basic elements of the profession. Nosser, a local judge, had studied geology as a young man, and was not unfamiliar with minerals and mineralization processes. One day, Nosser was poking around Carlisle's office looking at various ore samples when he found the blue quartz and the chicken bones. When he asked Carlisle about the items, he was told the story of Charley Wilson's discovery. Intrigued, Nosser studied the items and arrived at an interesting conclusion. The rock, he learned, was a blue, chalcedonic quartz containing tiny crystals of sylvanite. Searching his memory, Nosser recalled seeing such a rock in the past during one of his prospecting trips near Brown Mountain. The more Nosser thought about it, the more he became convinced that he had seen the same blue ledge from which Charley Wilson obtained his samples.

Encouraged by this information, Nosser, in the company of three friends, traveled to the Brown Mountain area and searched for several weeks in an attempt to find the gold-laden blue quartz. Though the expedition was unsuccessful, Nosser was sufficiently encouraged to undertake several more expeditions into the region.

During the next four years, Nosser traveled hundreds of miles and spent many days in the area between Brown Mountain and Searles Lake. Before his death, he told a close friend that he had narrowed down the location of the blue ledge of gold to a region about twenty miles northeast of Johannesburg and not far from the railroad loading dock at the small town of Trona.

Interest in the mysterious blue ledge continued for several years, and dozens have searched for it. It is possible, according to those who are familiar with the region, that the blue ledge, uncovered by a flash flood, may just as easily have been covered up again by soil deposits from a subsequent flow. In any event, the presumed site is now inside the boundaries of the China Lake Weapons Center, a fenced off territory unaccessible to civilians.

The Curse of the
Mormon Silver Ledge

SOMEWHERE IN FOLLY'S PASS in Death Valley's Panamint Range is a mysterious ledge of silver believed to carry a curse. The silver, estimated to be quite rich, proved to be difficult to obtain, for all who attempted to return for it died.

In early June, 1852, a large wagon train was being readied near Mountain Meadows, Utah, for a long journey to San Bernadino, California. The party consisted mostly of Mormons, but as the trail to California was known to be traveled by hostile Indians, several wagons piloted by gentiles were allowed to join to increase the size and safety of the party.

Most of the Mormons intended to settle in the San Bernadino area. They believed the fertile lands and the pleasant climate found there provided grand opportunities for farming, raising families, and building a church. The leaders of the wagon train decided to follow an old Spanish trail that wound somewhat erratically southward into Nevada before turning westward near the Colorado River and thence into California. When the fifty-nine wagons had completed preparations, the signal was given and the journey officially undertaken.

For weeks the lumbering wagons, pulled by oxen and mules, plodded onward, eventually reaching the drier regions of Nevada after several weeks. Locating water for passengers and livestock alike was a constant problem during this time of the year; many creeks lacked running water and several springs had dried up. For several days in a row rationing was required. The group was dangerously low on water when it finally arrived at Armagosa Springs, approximately seventy-five miles northwest of a cluster of some larger well-known springs near present-day Las Vegas. The party rested at Armagosa Springs for two days, but before all of the water barrels were filled, the spring's flow was exhausted. More than ever, the party now looked forward to arriving at the small oasis at Las Vegas Springs and resting livestock and travelers for several days while replenishing their water supply. The leaders of the wagon train, however, had other ideas. They decided to save time and distance by attempting a shortcut through a low pass in the Armagosa Range and picking up the main trail a few days later in California. This route, they claimed, would save about sixty miles and several days, but the likelihood of locating water along the way was not good. Loud and sometimes violent arguments soon broke out among members of the train about the competence of the leaders. Finally fifty of the wagons, organized under the command of a man named Smith, decided to continue on to the Las Vegas Springs. The remaining nine wagons left the trail and entered Death Valley, a land of little water, debilitating summer heat, and unfriendly Indians.

For a full day, the smaller wagon train progressed slowly across the arid wastes and finally stopped to camp along Furnace Creek where they found a trickle of water. Here another disagreement arose among the members, and in the morning seven of the wagons proceeded northwestward in the belief they would find abundant water in that direction. The remaining two wagons continued in a southwesterly direction following an old Indian trail that wound along the foothills of the Panamint Range.

Meanwhile, three members of the larger wagon train making its way to Las Vegas Springs tired of the continual discord that permeated the group. The three men—

Cadwallader, Farley, and Towne—believed they could make more efficient progress on their own, so they purchased a few supplies from the members of the party, filled their canteens and, on foot, started off across the waterless plain toward the west.

On the second day after leaving the main caravan, the three men began to regret their decision. With almost all of their water gone and no prospect of finding any, they were forced to endure the intense desert heat and blinding summer sun as they struggled onward. Finally, they reached Daylight Springs, a small oasis that provided some small amount of water and shade. After resting there for two days, they set out once again toward the west. Eventually, they came to the Panamint Range and entered Folly's Pass, intent on reaching the Panamint Valley on the western side.

As they hiked through the pass, the three travelers searched for a good place to camp for the night. Presently, Towne discovered a rock overhang large enough to accommodate their number and provide some shade. As Towne and Farley rested under the jutting overhang, Cadwallader volunteered to range about and hunt some rabbits for supper.

About seventy-five yards from their campsite, Cadwallader spotted a strikingly brilliant horizontal layer of rock along one wall of the canyon, a two foot thick ledge that gleamed brightly in the afternoon sun. On closer inspection, he was startled to discover it was a shelf of pink quartz containing a dense accumulation of silver. Cadwallader summoned his companions and moments later the three men regarded the shining ledge in awe.

Cadwallader, Farley, and Towne all had previous experience as miners and knew silver when they saw it. Staring at the silver-studded ledge before them, Towne remarked it was the richest ore of this kind he had ever seen. Excited, the three broke broke off several chunks of the ore and placed it in their packs. When they reached San Bernadino, they promised, they would mount an expedition and return to Folly's Pass to mine the silver.

The next morning the three travelers set out once again, braving the harsh desert that lay before them. On the third day after leaving the pass they arrived at Last Chance Spring where they found the two wagons that had separated from the group earlier. For several days Cadwallader, Farley, and Towne remained at the spring with the members of the small party.

One evening while seated around the campfire, the three men entered into a conversation with a traveler named King. King and his family, some of the few gentiles in the original party, were bound for Santa Clara where they intended to join relatives. At one point during the evening, Cadwallader pulled a piece of the silver-laden quartz out of his pocket and showed it to King. King, in turn, remarked that the ore was indeed very rich, the richest he had ever seen. When the three told King they wanted to organize an expedition in San Bernadino to return to Folly's Pass, he cautioned them that it might be difficult because everyone was investing in gold at the time. Gold, he explained, was worth more than silver.

Weeks later the small party finally arrived in San Bernadino. Cadwallader, Farley, and Towne immediately tried to interest some investors in returning to the Panamint Range to mine the silver, but discovered that King's observations had been correct: Everyone was interested only in gold. Discouraged, the three friends eventually separated and pursued different opportunities. Cadwallader invested in some mining interests in Mexico, while Farley and Towne settled in Los Angeles.

About a year and a half after surviving their perilous trek through the desert, Farley and Towne finally convinced a group of investors in Los Angeles to join them in a silver mining venture in the Panamint Range. Skeptical at first, the investors were finally convinced when shown some of the silver taken from the ledge in Folly's Pass. A subsequent assay undertaken by one of them proved the ore to be extremely rich, so rich that they all believed a great profit could be made from establishing a mine. Several weeks later, with Farley as their guide, a small group of well-provisioned, well-mounted, and well-armed men left Los Angeles bound for the Panamints.

When they reached the pass, disaster struck almost immediately. On the first night in camp, Farley got into an argument with one of the investors who responded by shooting him through the heart, killing him instantly. Without Farley to lead them to the ledge of silver, the group had no choice but to return to Los Angeles. The ledge had claimed its first victim.

On returning to Los Angeles, the investors sought out Towne, explained the death of Farley, and asked him to lead a second expedition to find the silver. Towne initially balked at the idea, but eventually agreed to join the group. The party was in its third day of the second expedition to Folly's Pass when Towne became seriously ill with food poisoning and died.

Frustrated at the deaths of the two men who could lead them to the mine, the investors were about to abandon the project when someone suggested they locate Cadwallader and lure him into the enterprise. Several weeks later, Cadwallader was found and brought to Los Angeles where he agreed, for a price, to guide the party to the silver ledge.

Since Cadwallader had moved to Mexico, he had abandoned most of the tenets of the Mormon religion and had become a heavy drinker. During the third expedition to the Panamint Range, Cadwallader drank constantly and had a difficult time remaining in the saddle. While only a day away from Folly's Pass, Cadwallader died, presumably from an overdose of alcohol.

Believing the silver ledge discovered over two years earlier by the three Mormons was cursed, the investors returned to Los Angeles and never again attempted to locate it.

In 1857, a man named Bailey organized yet another expedition to find the cursed silver ledge of the Mormons, as it came to be known. An explorer, trapper, and Indian fighter, Bailey claimed to be intimate with Death Valley and the Panamint Range and stated to one and all he could find the ledge of silver with no trouble. After collecting $75,000 from investors, Bailey disappeared and rumors later surfaced that his body, scalped and mutilated, was found alongside some remote trail deep in the heart of Death Valley.

About a year following Bailey's misfortune, a prospector named Buel decided to search for the silver. Buel heard the tale of the cursed ledge while in Los Angeles and, after locating and talking to King in Santa Clara, believed he could retrace the route of Cadwallader, Farley, and Towne into Folly's Pass. Alone, he traveled to the Panamints leading two burros piled high with supplies.

A year later, Buel was found by a party of hunters on the road to Austin, Nevada, some eighty miles northeast of the Panamints. Buel claimed he had found the cursed silver ledge of the Mormons, showed his rescuers several small pieces of rich silver, and promptly died.

The story of the cursed silver ledge of the Mormons became well known throughout California and others took up the search. Each expedition, however, met with failure and quite often with disaster and death.

The silver ledge is still there, located deep in Folly's Pass and still gleaming brightly in the desert sun. Some are still tantalized by the tale of the lost silver, but most refrain from entering this arid and forbidden land.

Many who have been tempted to search for the silver ledge bring up the notion of the curse. Most claim they do not believe in such things, but they still stay away from Folly's Pass.

Golden Gravels of Goler Wash

AMONG THE THOUSANDS WHO JOURNEYED west to California with hopes of striking it rich in the gold fields were two Germans, John Goler and John Graff. Like the others, they carried little save for their few belongings and their dreams. The dreams of Goler and Graff were realized for short time, for they accidentally discovered a rich deposit of gold in some remote canyon in the Panamint Ridge only to lose it. Sixty-seven years later, using vague directions provided by Goler, the canyon was rediscovered and the streambed gravels at the bottom of it eventually yielded over one million dollars worth of gold.

Goler and Graff migrated from Germany to the United States sometime during the early 1840s. Blacksmiths by trade, both men had gained some mining experience in Europe. On arriving in America, they sought similar opportunities. The two men eventually drifted into the Georgia Appalachians where they alternately prospected for gold on their own and worked for large mining companies.

In 1849, Goler and Graff learned of the gold strike in California and longed to journey westward to try their luck. In the spring of 1850, the two Germans joined a party of gold-seekers who were organizing a wagon train to travel to California and dig for gold. Pooling their meager savings, Goler and Graff bought passage. As they made the slow and sometimes arduous journey across the country, their spirits remained buoyed with thoughts of striking it rich. Many weeks later, the wagon train arrived in Las Vegas, Nevada, at the time a well-known junction of frequently traveled roads where weary migrants could find freshwater springs. Several days later, the wagon train continued on to California, skirting the southern edge of Death Valley.

After entering California, Goler and Graff occasionally drifted away from the wagon train to explore the area and examine promising rock outcrops. Each day they wandered farther from the group until one afternoon they became lost and were unable to relocate the group. With nothing more than the packs they carried on their backs, a canteen of water apiece, and an old Spencer repeating rifle owned by Goler, the two Germans set out across the Panamint Range, hoping to intersect the trail on the western side and rejoin the wagon train.

For three days the two men wandered through canyons and over ridges. Having exhausted the meager supply of food they carried, the two supplemented their diet with lizards and snakes they managed to kill until Goler ran out of ammunition. Luck was with them, however, for they encountered several freshwater springs at which they filled their canteens.

Late afternoon of the third day in the range, the exhausted Germans sought shade in the shelter of an overhanging rock in the lower part of a canyon that opened into the Panamint Valley to the west. They had drank the last of their water earlier that morning and tired, hungry, and thirsty, they sought rest and refuge from the burning midday sun. Reposing beneath the rocky ledge, the two men scanned the canyon floor in search of some evidence of a spring. Finding none, Graff decided to climb down to the dry stream at the bottom of the canyon to try to locate water by digging into the streambed, a technique the local Indians often employed. Goler remained in the shade.

After about fifteen minutes of scooping a shallow hole in the stream gravels, Graff excitedly called to Goler to come down to the wash, that he had discovered gold and plenty of it. Forgetting his exhaustion and hunger, John Goler joined his friend, and together the two men marveled at the quantity of large gold nuggets lying about in the gravels of the wash.

As the friends picked nuggets from the streambed, a rare summer thundershower brought rain to the canyon, and here and there small basins in the rock partially filled with small amounts of water. Using this source to keep their nagging thirst at bay, Goler and Graff worked for two days extracting an impressive amount of gold nuggets from the sun-bleached gravels. After accumulating several pounds of gold apiece, they realized they would never be able to transport their heavy treasure across the arid Panamint Valley, so they searched about for a suitable hiding place, intending to return for it. After several minutes of searching, Graff discovered a deep, narrow crevice in a nearby ledge into which they stuffed the gold. After plugging the crevice with some common rocks, Goler climbed a nearby hill and stuck the barrel of his rifle into the ground at the top to serve as a marker. Following this, the two men hoisted their packs and struck out toward the west.

Goler and Graff were never able to relocate the wagon train or the trail, and after wandering lost for several weeks, eventually arrived in Los Angeles. Penniless, both men sought jobs. They planned to save enough money together to outfit a pack train to return to the golden gravels of the remote canyon in the Panamint Range. Goler immediately found work in a local blacksmith shop and Graff secured employment with a tailor. Months passed, and the two friends slowly added to their savings as they dreamed of returning to retrieve their gold.

One morning Goler learned that his friend Graff had been killed. Saddened at the loss of his longtime companion, Goler sought emotional refuge in the solitude of his work.

Two years passed, and Goler's dreams of returning to the canyon in the Panamint Range gradually gave way to other endeavors. Soon the German established a blacksmith shop of his own, and with time he became a successful and prosperous businessman.

As he grew older, Goler's thoughts often returned to the wealth of gold nuggets he and Graff had found long ago in the remote canyon on the Panamint Range. Longing to return, and believing he could still locate the canyon, Goler assembled a party consisting of a few friends and together they traveled to the Panamint Range. Time, however, worked to the disadvantage of Goler, for when he arrived in the general region he realized he no longer remembered anything about the range and could not recognize important landmarks. After several such trips, he finally abandoned his hopes of finding the canyon and recovering the gold.

When he was an old man, Goler related the story of the discovery of gold to his friend Grant Cuddeback, a successful rancher who maintained large herds of cattle on several sections of land near Los Angeles. Cuddeback, a man with a keen sense of adventure, encouraged Goler to tell him everything he remembered about the canyon containing the gold-filled gravels. Finally, equipped with Goler's tale and a crudely drawn map, the rancher financed a large group of men to search for the mysterious canyon.

After three attempts to find the canyon over the next two years, Cuddeback finally discovered it. In 1917, while exploring some promising canyons that opened into the Panamint Valley, Cuddeback spurred his mount to the top of a low hill in order to obtain a better view of a wash he was interested in exploring. As he dismounted, his attention was distracted by the presence of a very old, rusted rifle sticking out of the ground nearby. Cuddeback examined it and saw that it was Golers' Spencer repeater. Below him in the canyon, he realized, lay the golden gravels of which the old German spoke.

Though he searched for two full days, Cuddeback and his followers could not locate the crevice into which Goler and Graff cached the nuggets they took from the gravels. They did, however, find hundreds of large nuggets in the rocky wash of what Cuddeback named Goler Wash.

Cuddeback returned to Los Angeles where he formed a mining company. Within a few weeks, he had employed engineers and laborers, and returned to the canyon. For the next three years, Cuddeback's workers dug in the gravels of Goler Wash, eventually extracting over a million dollars in gold.

Even today, Goler Wash is not easily accessible. The hardy explorer who manages to reach this remote location, however, may discover a few nuggets overlooked by the miners who worked this area over seventy years earlier. In 1972, one modern day prospector who spent almost a week in the canyon returned to his Los Angeles home with more than a dozen such nuggets, each weighing approximately five ounces.

Indian Treasure
in the Argus Mountains

SOMEWHERE NOT FAR FROM LAMOTTE SPRING in Death Valley's Argus Mountains lies a little known treasure cave. As recently as sixty years ago, the cave was known to some area Indians who believed their ancestors used it to store precious artifacts along with some gold. After being shown several large gold nuggets purportedly taken from the cave, one man searched for and found it, but when he returned to town to obtain ropes necessary for entering the cave, he suffered a serious accident which prevented his return. During the years since his death, the mysterious cave has eluded searchers, and today its location may fall within protected federal property.

During the latter part of the 1920s, there were very few profitable ore claims left to be obtained in the southern part of California. In spite of that fact, many prospectors still explored remote areas in the waterless wastes far from settlements and well-traveled roads, hoping someday to make a long-dreamed of strike.

One such prospector was Frank Bishop, a desert-hardened fortune-seeker who had devoted most of his adult life to examining promising outcrops in the southernmost extension of the Argus Range, an ancient mass of intrusive volcanic rock located not far from the town of Trona. In spite of his advanced age Bishop, well-supplied with food and equipment, often spent several weeks at a time in the rugged Argus Canyons prospecting for an elusive deposit of valuable ore. When not searching for gold, Bishop resided in an old weathered frame house just outside the town of Brown, some fifteen miles southwest of the Argus Range.

One cold February evening, Bishop was settled in next to his blazing hearth reading some month-old newspapers when he heard a knock on the door. An intensely private man, almost reclusive, Bishop grudgingly rose to answer the rapping and was surprised to be greeted by an old friend, an Indian he had known for several years.

Bishop offered his guest some hot tea and sometime during the evening as the two men talked, the Indian pulled a necklace from his pack and showed it to the old prospector. As Bishop examined the necklace, it became clear to him that it was exquisitely made yet quite old. For the most part it consisted of shell beads of various colors, but descending as pendants from the front were three acorn-sized gold nuggets!

When Bishop inquired about the origin of the necklace, the Indian told him he had found it in a cave located near a spring in the southern end of the Argus Mountains. The cave, according to the Indian, contained an untold number of artifacts similar to the neckpiece Bishop held in his hand and was apparently used by ancient dwellers of this part of California long before the time of his tribe. When the ancients left, they stored many of their belongings inside the cave, believing they would be protected until sometime in the future when the tribe might be able to return, but they never did. Before departing Bishop's cabin, the Indian provided Bishop with directions to the cave and cautioned the prospector that it was difficult and dangerous to enter.

Several days later, Bishop completed preparations for a journey to the cave. Using the directions given to him by the Indian, he arrived at Lamotte Spring, a water hole well known to area prospectors. Here he set up a temporary camp and began to explore the nearby canyons and ridges.

For several days Bishop searched the environs for the

cave described by the Indian but was unable to locate it. As he explored the adjacent desert and mountain country, Bishop discovered several vertical rock walls which contained numerous petroglyphs, all of which were evidently very old, testimony to an ancient tribe's habitation of the region.

Unable to locate the cave, Bishop turned his attention to prospecting for gold and dismissed the tale of the fabulous cache of precious artifacts. For the next two years, he searched the area for the cave when he found himself nearby, but he gradually began to believe his Indian friend had made up the entire story. And then one day while Bishop was inspecting the surface of a rounded weathered granite ridge, he found it!

As Bishop made his way across the top of the great mass of exposed gray rock not far from the spring, he spotted a wide opening in the rock yawning at him from several dozen feet below. Carefully inching his way down the steep slope of the granite outcrop, the prospector approached the wide orifice and peered into the dim interior. Rather than a natural cavern, the cave was a huge cleft in the mountain, most likely caused by a violent earthquake millions of years earlier. The entrance was entirely vertical and the walls were sheer, with no footholds or handholds whatsoever. Since Bishop had no rope to facilitate descent, he could only peer into the depths of the great fracture.

As the sun gradually made its way to a point nearly overhead, rays of light illuminated portions of the interior of the cleft far below where Bishop perched on the edge. Deep within, he could see several old baskets stacked against one wall. Bishop also believed he caught the reflection of sunlight off golden artifacts lying scattered about the floor of the cave though he wasn't certain.

For the rest of the day, Bishop searched the area for an alternate entrance to the treasure-filled room he imagined existed deep in the cave. When he found none, he decided to return to Brown to replenish his supplies and purchase several stout ropes.

While in Brown, Bishop suffered a severe accident in which he shattered his right femur in several places. The break was a bad one, and for a time the physician who treated the old man was unsure if it would heal properly or if the old man would ever walk again. For several weeks Bishop was confined to bed, and when he was finally allowed to get about on his own, he required the use of crutches. Just moving from one room to another in his small house was difficult and painful for the aging prospector, and he found the healing process interminably long and exasperating. During his recovery period, Bishop constantly thought about the fortune in golden artifacts lying on the floor of the remote cave in the Argus Range.

As the time passed and Bishop's leg slowly repaired itself, the old man caught pneumonia and was hospitalized once again. For another two weeks he was bedridden and nearly at the point of death when he was visited by his daughter. Ignoring the old man's pleas to be left alone, the daughter had him moved to her home in Los Angeles where she nursed him until he passed away three years later.

Frank Bishop was never able to return to the treasure cave he found in the Argus Range, a cave he believed until his dying day held a fortune in gold artifacts most likely cached by Indians long ago. While taking some afternoon sun on the front lawn of his daughter's home in Los Angeles, Bishop provided directions to the treasure cave to a young man who befriended him, but when he traveled to the Argus Range to search for it several weeks later, the man found the directions vague and unreliable. When he returned to California to obtain additional information from Bishop, he learned the old man had died.

Because of its remoteness, aridity, and the dense population of rattlesnakes, the Argus Range was never particularly attractive to prospectors. Even hikers generally avoided the area. After Bishop's death, others learned of his find and made attempts to locate the mysterious treasure cave, but all came away disappointed.

There is no reason to doubt Bishop's claim of a treasure cached deep in a wide cleft in these mountains. His deathbed assertion that it existed was convincing for many, and Bishop had nothing to gain by perpetrating a lie. Finding the cave today, however, has been made extremely difficult, if not impossible because the China Lake Naval Weapons Center now encompasses most of the Argus Range and the presumed location of the lost treasure cave.

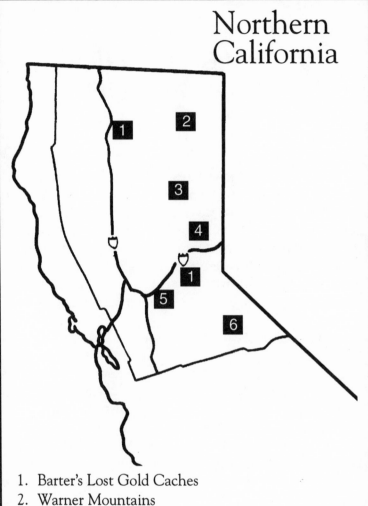

Northern California

1. Barter's Lost Gold Caches
2. Warner Mountains
3. Lost Lake of Gold
4. Hobo Camp Gold
5. Calaveras County Gold
6. Lost Cement Mine

Gold Cache in the Warner Mountains

EAGLE PEAK IS A PROMINENT LANDMARK in northern California's Warner Mountains. In one of the canyons that extends from Eagle Peak is a shallow cave, the front of which is partially closed off by crudely built rock wall. Over a century ago, a Pit River Indian lived in this cave along with several hundred pounds of gold ore stolen from a freight wagon. The Indian was beaten to death by four men determined to learn the location of the gold, but the secret died with him.

In March of 1881, a freight wagon carrying several hundred pounds of gold ore was being driven from the Black Rock mining region of Nevada to Sacramento, California. The road, commonly used by travelers and freighters, wound through high mountain passes and across low, wide plains. As the wagon, accompanied by three armed guards, passed by the southern edge of the Warner Mountains near Moon Lake, a lone rider approached. Perceiving the newcomer as a fellow traveler, the guards waved a friendly greeting and reined up to inquire about conditions along the trail farther south. As he neared the wagon escorts the stranger, quick as lightning, pulled a rifle from beneath his poncho and blasted two of the guards from their saddles. The remaining escort and the driver of the wagon threw their hands in the air and immediately surrendered.

The robber, his face hidden by a wide-brimmed hat pulled low over his face and the fold of his thick poncho pulled up to his nose, ordered the two remaining members of the party to begin walking toward the nearest settlement, some twenty miles to the south. Once the men had covered about a hundred yards, the bandit tied his horse to the tail-gate of the freight wagon, climbed into the seat, and whipped the lead animals northward at a fast pace. With a calmness belying his crime, the lone outlaw steered the shipment of gold to a predetermined location in a remote canyon in the west side of the Warner Mountains where he intended to cache it. Thus did Holden Dick, a somewhat reclusive Indian, come into possession of a fortune in gold ore.

Holden Dick was a member of the Pit River tribe, a small, poverty-ridden assemblage of hunter-gatherers who lived a few miles southeast of Alturas. Holden Dick's needs were simple—he desired only a roof over his head and a full belly. It galled him to visit Alturas and observe whites living in relative splendor on former Indian lands while he and members of his tribe starved. He was twenty-seven years of age when, fed up with poverty, he committed the robbery of the ore-laden freight wagon.

Holden Dick cached the gold ore in a shallow shelter cave located deep in one of the canyons that was incised into the western slope of the southern part of the Warner Mountains. The Indian constructed a crude rock wall across a portion of the cave entrance and lived in this makeshift shelter throughout most of the year. Occasionally, however, he ventured into the towns of Alturas and Susanville where he obtained supplies and idled away evenings in one of the many taverns found in those settlements. When he purchased provisions, he always paid for them with gold ore. Because he normally carried only small amounts of the ore at a time, most people believed Holden Dick was working a poor mining claim someplace back up in the mountains.

One day Holden Dick carried an unusually heavy pack into a tavern in Susanville, a pack from which he pulled a handful of almost pure gold ore which he used to pay for his drinks. Several men playing cards at a nearby table saw the gleam of the gold and invited the Indian to join them. Holden Dick politely refused but bought drinks for the entire group. While fielding questions from the curious men, he admitted the pack was filled with ore, but refused to respond to questions about its origin. A day or two later, Holden Dick loaded some newly purchased supplies onto a spare horse and rode northward toward the Warner Mountains.

Holden Dick had reached the southern limit of the Madeline Plains around noon when he discovered he was being followed. Even though the trackers were nearly a half-mile away, the Indian recognized two of them as the card players who had asked him several questions about his gold. That evening, Holden Dick stopped for camp, built a fire, and laid out his bedroll, all within sight of the group of men who watched him from a ravine some distance away. When the trackers were certain the Indian had bedded down for the night, they retreated about a half-mile and set up their own camp. Holden Dick extinguished his fire after about two hours and waited patiently. Then, very quietly yet with remarkable efficiency, he loaded his gear and rode away.

Holden Dick was followed on several other occasions while returning to the Warner Mountains from Susanville. Once a party of trackers had trailed the Indian to the mouth of the very canyon in which his secret cache was located, but Holden Dick hid in the rocks and shot and killed one of them as they rode up the trail, a man named Samuel B. Shaw.

In March, 1885, Holden Dick was riding into Susanville when he was approached by Sheriff C.C. Rachford. Rachford arrested the Indian for the murder of Shaw and placed him in the jail at Susanville. Several weeks later a trial was held, Holden Dick was convicted of murder, and the judge sentenced him to hang by the neck until dead. Several appeals were filed, and it was nearly ten months later when a new trial date was finally set.

On the evening of January 23, 1886, Holden Dick sat in his jail cell contemplating his chances in the upcoming trial. At the same time a group of men who coveted the Indian's gold were busy hatching a plot they believed would make them rich. Late that same night, the men succeeded in gaining access to Holden Dick's cell and offered to free him if he would tell them where the gold was hidden. Surprisingly, the Indian refused, saying he would rather hang than reveal the secret location of his gold cache.

Enraged, the four men unlocked the cell and dragged Holden Dick out into the street. In the darkness of the overcast night, they threatened to kill the Pit River Indian unless he told them where the gold was hidden. Holden Dick continued to refuse, even spitting in the face of one of his captors. Angered, the man beat the Indian mercilessly. For the next hour, Holden Dick was interrogated, whipped, and tortured, finally dying at the hands of the men who would have his fortune.

Frustrated and angry, the gang dragged Holden Dick's body into a nearby blacksmith shop and hanged it from a rope tied to a rafter.

Few today know of the story of Holden Dick's lost gold cache, but those that do claim the treasure is hidden in a cave located somewhere in a canyon that extends toward Eagle Peak, a prominent landmark in the southern part of the Warner Mountains.

Outlaw Barter's
Lost Gold Caches

THOUGH LACKING THE NOTORIETY of other more colorful
California bandits of the mid-nineteenth century, Richard
Barter proved to be an effective robber, amassing nearly a
million dollars in cash, coins, and gold. Most of this fortune
is thought to have been buried near Folsom, California,
though a second cache of $50,000, taken in a robbery mas-
terminded by Barter, was buried in a remote canyon of
Trinity Mountain of Shasta County. To this day, none of
Barter's caches are known to have been located.

Richard Barter was born in Canada, the son of a British
military officer. He was a young man when he began to hear
the stories of the great gold strikes in northern California,
and he dreamed of traveling to that far western state to make
his fortune. When his father passed away a short time later,
Barter, along with four relatives, moved to California. They
eventually drifted to the Sierra Nevada Range in Placer
County and settled into a canyon cut by the North Fork of
the American River. Because several placer miners had filed
claims nearby, Barter and his party decided to try their luck
panning for gold in the glacially fed stream.

For the next several months, the members of the group
worked hard but panned only enough gold to barely keep
them fed. Eventually, they drifted away leaving only Barter
to work the small claim.

For supplies, Barter would occasionally travel to the

nearby settlement of Auburn, and while there he would spend a couple of days drinking with friends in a tavern. Most of Auburn's citizens admired the young man for sticking to his poor claim, and they perceived him as a hard worker and congenial fellow.

As Barter was leading his supply-laded burro out of Auburn one day in 1853, a group of lawmen led by Deputy Sheriff John Boggs surrounded him and placed him under arrest. As Barter was being escorted to the jail, Boggs informed him the owner of the town's mercantile had charged him with stealing some merchandise.

When word of the arrest got around town, several of Barter's friends raised some money and bailed him out. They obtained a lawyer for him and the charge was eventually dropped.

Approximately three months later, Barter was arrested again as he rode into Auburn, this time on a charge of stealing a mule. He was tried and quickly sentenced to two years in prison, but just as he was being led from the jail to the awaiting carriage which was to transport him to the penitentiary, the real mule thief confessed to the crime. Though Barter was released, many of the area residents began to regard him as a thief. Soon, placer miners in the area of Barter's camp were accusing him of encroaching onto their claims. Shots were occasionally fired into Barter's camp at night and the young man decided it was time to move elsewhere.

Barter eventually migrated to the town of Redding in Shasta County, about 150 miles to the north, where he worked at odd jobs. One day an Auburn businessman arrived in Redding, recognized Barter, and spread the story that he was a thief and not to be trusted. After that, Barter found it difficult to find work and, ironically, decided to turn to crime to make a living.

For the next several months, Barter robbed lone travelers along the remote roads and trails in Shasta County.

When he tired of this, he would raid small placer camps and take whatever gold he could obtain.

Taking money from unarmed travelers and miners was easy as well as lucrative, and as time passed Barter accumulated a sizeable fortune in gold, cash, and coins. It grew to the degree that the young outlaw stuffed it into saddlebags and transported it on a pack mule. His wandering and outlaw ways eventually took him back to Auburn, and for several more months he regularly waylaid wayfarers and peddlers along the road that led from Auburn to Folsom, about twenty miles to the south. Following each robbery, Barter would retreat to an old abandoned ramshackle cabin he moved into just outside of Folsom. Here he buried his loot, keeping out only a small amount for himself.

Barter's success and subsequent reputation began to attract other outlaws, and soon a gang consisting of about five or six desperadoes led by the young robber was terrorizing citizens, farmers, and businessmen throughout Placer County. After each successful robbery, Barter paid off his men and placed his share of the loot into his growing cache buried somewhere near the cabin.

As the robberies between Auburn and Folsom continued, Deputy Sheriff Boggs was given the job of tracking down the outlaws and bringing them to justice. Boggs was the arresting officer on Barter's first two charges and the two men subsequently grew to hate each other. Boggs was heard to state on several occasions that he would just as soon bring Barter in dead as alive.

When Barter learned that Boggs was tracking him, his response was to increase his efforts to rob not only travelers, but also farmers, settlers, and even churches. His activities took him as far north as Nevada City. Boggs interpreted Barter's boldness as a challenge, and he placed greater effort into apprehending the young bandit. As Boggs pursued Barter, the latter made plans for his biggest robbery ever.

Barter learned that a shipment of gold was being readied near Yreka, a mining camp near the Oregon border. Because roads were poor, the gold bullion, worth $80,000, was being loaded onto mules which were to be driven to Redding where it would be transferred to wagons and shipped to Sacramento. Barter, familiar with the region from his days in Shasta County, decided to attack the mule train where the trail passed Trinity Mountain. Here the terrain was rough and rugged and afforded an excellent opportunity for surprise and escape.

At the last minute, Barter learned that the mules used to transport the gold all bore a large and obvious brand that identified them as property of the mining company. Not wanting to be caught with the easily recognizable animals, Barter decided to transfer the gold onto a string of unbranded mules immediately after the robbery and turn the mining company stock loose. To this end, he assigned three members of his gang to rob the pack train and cache the gold at a secret location while he and another gang member returned to Auburn to obtain the replacement mules.

As the pack train, guarded by only four armed escorts, slowly traversed the rock-strewn, twisting trail near Trinity Mountain, the three gang members attacked it. The surprised guards immediately surrendered and the bandits tied them up and left them on the trail. Leading the mules deep into a remote canyon, they unloaded the gold and buried it in a location they had selected the previous day. While one of the outlaws herded the branded mules out of the canyon, the other two set up a temporary camp near the gold to await the return of Barter and the replacement stock. Unknown to the outlaws, however, Barter and his companion had been arrested by Boggs as they attempted to steal a half dozen mules from a farmer in Auburn.

On the second day following the robbery, one of the outlaws guarding the gold discovered the guards had broken free and escaped. It would be only a matter of another day or two when lawmen would arrive to search the area, so the robbers decided they could remain no longer. The outlaws took what gold they were able to carry, approximately $10,000 each, and reburied the rest. From Trinity Mountain, they rode southeastward toward Folsom and the old cabin where they expected to find Barter.

Days later when the three men rode up to the cabin, they were unaware that Bogg's and five posse members were waiting for them inside. As the outlaws unsaddled their mounts, gunfire erupted from the cabin killing two of the outlaws outright and wounding the third. The surviving bandit was given a quick trial and sentenced to life in prison where he died from consumption a short time later. Now there was no one left alive who knew the location of the buried cache of gold bullion at Trinity Mountain.

While awaiting trial, Barter escaped from the county jail and fled to San Francisco where he remained hidden for several months. About two years later, he formed a new gang and returned to the business of robbing travelers along the Nevada City-Auburn-Folsom road. After each robbery, Barter continued to place his share of the loot into his growing hoard buried near his cabin.

Late one afternoon, Barter and a companion, having just robbed a family of several thousand dollars near Auburn, were returning to Folsom along a seldom-used trail. Unknown to the outlaws, Boggs had learned of the robbery, quickly formed a posse, and set out in pursuit. Riding up on the bandits from behind, Boggs called out for them to surrender. In response, Barter raised a pistol and fired at the lawmen. A brief gunfight ensued and Barter was shot twice in the chest, killed instantly.

In addition to the $50,000 in gold bullion hidden in some remote canyon near Trinity Mountain in Shasta County, it is estimated that Dick Barter had cached around $200,000 in cash, coin, and gold at a secret location in the yard of his old cabin near Folsom. The treasures, likely worth far in excess of a million dollars today, remain lost.

Lake of Gold

For well over one hundred years, a legend concerning a lake of gold has circulated around northern California, a fantastic tale of great quantities of rich ore lying only inches below a clear blue body of water far from well-traveled trails.

Several have encountered this lake and returned with impressive amounts of gold and descriptions of the small body of water not much larger than a pond. Others have searched for the lake only to return with nothing save discouragement. And many more ponder the existence of this near-mythical lake and the fortune in large gold nuggets reflecting from the bottom.

During the frenzied gold rush of 1849, no one was more surprised at the hysteria than an old trapper named Caleb Greenwood. Greenwood lived in a log cabin just outside of Placerville, which was called Dry Diggings at that time. When the miners showed the old man the gold they took from the rock and the stream bottoms, Greenwood remained puzzled at their excitement and told them he had seen much larger nuggets several years earlier lying plentifully about in a small lake located high in the Sierras. When the miners offered Greenwood a large fee to guide them to the lake he refused, but informed the men that his son, John, would show them where it was. A week later, John Greenwood, carrying a map prepared by Caleb, led a party of thirteen miners up a long, winding trail high into the mountains. On the second day, Caleb's map proved difficult to follow, and the young Greenwood became lost several times. In all, a month was spent in the mountains in search of the lake of gold but, though many lakes were found, none contained any ore.

Discouraged, the miners finally returned, but the story of the lost lake of gold began to spread among the growing communities springing up in this part of California.

*   *   *

By the summer of 1850, thousands of mining claims had been filed and millions of dollars' worth of gold was being taken each day from the shafts and the placer mines that abounded throughout this region. In June of that year, a Scandinavian named Lingard arrived in the area to try his luck at mining. As he wandered among the many placer claims along Soldier's Gulch and Grass Valley, Lingard, who had considerable mining experience, wondered about the source of all this gold, the lode of exposed ore at some location higher in the mountains that yielded the precious nuggets that had been washed down to these lower altitudes over the previous eons. Believing that such an incredible deposit must exist somewhere high above the placer mines, Lingard was determined to search for it.

After several weeks of following the gold-laden streams to their sources in the mountains, Lingard came upon a small lake near which he made camp. Overflow from this lake from melting snow and glaciers washed over a low rock rim and fed a tiny stream that ran along the floor of a sizeable canyon below. This particular stream had attracted hundreds of placer miners who were each taking as much as six and seven hundred dollars worth of gold per day from the gravelly bottom. As Lingard explored around the lake, he encountered evidence of ages-old intrusive volcanic activity, the type that is often associated with the formation of gold.

One afternoon as Lingard filled his coffeepot with water from the clear blue lake, his attention was drawn to a glimmer just below the cool, rippling surface. Scooping up some of the bottom gravel and sand, Lingard's heart raced as he picked out several large gold nuggets. Another half-hour of examining the bottom of the small lake near the margins yielded a total of six pounds of gold.

After placing the nuggets in his pack, Lingard left the mountain and traveled northward to the town of Downieville. Here he attempted to organize a party of men to return with him to the lake and undertake a large scale mining operation. After showing them the examples of almost pure gold he took from the lake, approximately twenty miners agreed to participate in the venture. As Lingard's party purchased supplies and readied their equipment during the next few days, word leaked out of the Scandinavian's discovery and the purpose of the expedition. In response, the price of mining equipment and supplies as well as mules and horses rose dramatically. Worse, as Lingard's group departed Downieville, they were followed by an estimated 200 men, each intent on learning the location of the lake of gold.

For weeks, Lingard's party attempted to evade the trailing horde. Shots were occasionally fired and at least one death was recorded. To complicate matters, Lingard became lost several times in search of the lake and his followers began to bicker and grumble about his leadership. Several more days passed and half of the original party abandoned the expedition.

As Lingard's party entered the Sierras around the beginning of the autumn season, they were occasionally pelted with snowfall. Once into the high country, however, snow storms were plentiful and made traveling difficult. More time was spent on the trail and in camp than anticipated and consequently food supplies ran critically low. To make matters worse, Lingard admitted he was lost and unable to find the lake. Enraged, the miners threatened to hang their leader, but eventually just abandoned him and returned to Downieville.

For several years thereafter, Lingard searched for the lake of gold from which he retrieved the impressive nuggets, but was never able to relocate it.

* * *

A few months following the break-up of the Lingard expedition, the son of a wealthy South American shipping magnate arrived in San Francisco to handle some of his father's business concerns. While visiting a tavern one evening, the young man chanced to meet a fellow drinker who related a remarkable story.

The new friend told the young businessman he had overheard a conversation among some miners in a saloon in Sacramento wherein they described a lost lake of gold high in the Sierra Nevada Mountains to the east. Being familiar with the country of which the miners spoke, the man outfitted himself and a partner and undertook a search for the lake. Several weeks later they discovered it, and over the next four months carried several burro loads of gold ore from the site into Sacramento. The two men became wealthy and purchased several businesses in the town.

* * *

During the spring of 1850, a placer miner named Marks (or Marx) was working his claim one afternoon when he was visited by an Indian, a member of a tribe which lived in the mountains north of the Yuba River.

When Marks showed the visitor some of the gold he had panned from the icy stream, the Indian, unimpressed, pulled several large gold nuggets from his pack and gave them to the miner. Astounded at the size and quality of the ore, Marks asked the Indian where they came from, and was provided with a description of a small lake high in the mountains where the nuggets lay about the bottom in profusion.

Marks enlisted the help of a businessman named John Rose, and together the two assembled a party of about two dozen men to enter the mountains and search for the lake of gold. After weeks of wandering through the high country trying to follow the directions provided by the Indian, the men could find nothing and finally gave up and returned.

* * *

One day during the late spring of 1850, a man named Stoddard stumbled into a mining camp located not far from Downieville with an incredible story.

Stoddard was a member of a wagon train which had entered California some seven months earlier, bound for Oregon. The party was camped near a place called Big Meadows, some forty miles to the north of Downieville. The emigrants decided to remain at the camp for several days to rest livestock and travelers alike, and Stoddard and another man were sent out to hunt game.

For two days the men searched for sign of wild game but found none. Their ranging took them several miles to the south into the forest-cloaked higher altitudes where they finally succeeded in killing a large bear. Having considerably more meat than they could carry, Stoddard and his companion cut several choice pieces and made preparations to return to the wagon train when snow began to fall. As they proceeded in the general direction from which they came, the snowfall grew heavier and the narrow game trail was eventually obliterated by a carpet of white. By nightfall, Stoddard and his companion were hopelessly lost.

After spending a sleepless night in a shallow cave, the two men traveled west the following morning, determined to follow the drainage out of the mountain in the hope of locating a settlement in the foothills below. Within minutes after leaving the cave, they came upon a small lake about ten acres in size, its blue waters offering a sharp contrast to the snow-covered landscape. As the men drank their fill from the clear pool, Stoddard spotted large gold nuggets lying just below the surface. Excited, he picked several of them from the gravel, eventually filling his jacket pockets with the rich gold. Walking around the margin of the lake, the two men saw considerably more gold glittering from the lake bottom.

Stoddard, not a stranger to mining and mineral formation, noticed that the small lake was in a shallow depression, the kind often scoured out of bedrock by the erosive action of a former glacier. The resultant basin, called a cirque, was the product of the removal of tons of rock. As the granite was abraded away by the ice, a rich gold-bearing seam of quartz was exposed. Over time, perhaps hundreds of thousands of years, the quartz eroded, releasing the chunks of gold contained therein and depositing them along the bottom of the cirque.

Stoddard also noted that along the far end of the lake was a steep cliff, quite weathered and laced with fractures and clefts, likely the result of previous earthquakes.

As the two men discussed their amazing discovery, they were suddenly attacked by Indians. They fled from the area, but Stoddard's companion was struck by an arrow and fell. Stoddard, unaware that his friend had been hit, continued to run as fast as he could. Several minutes later the sounds of the screaming Indians had subsided and the frightened man stopped to rest. Looking around, Stoddard saw no sign of his companion and presumed he had been killed.

For months, Stoddard wandered around the mountains, lost and existing on such roots, fruits, and small game as he could find. By the time he stumbled out of the range and into Downieville, he was haggard, half-crazed, and suffered extreme frostbite.

It took several weeks for Stoddard to fully recover from his ordeal, but as soon as he was able to travel he made preparations to return to the range and retrieve a fortune in gold from the lake.

Enlisting about a dozen men to accompany him into the mountains, Stoddard spent the next several years trying to find to the lake of gold but with no success. Though he arrived at a location where he was certain he had seen the lake, it was nowhere to be found. Confused and dejected, he abandoned the search.

In 1853, a mining engineer named Roberts became intrigued by the tale of the lost lake of gold. He eventually acquired locational information from Stoddard, and in the summer of that year entered the mountains with the hope of finding the elusive water-filled cirque.

According to Roberts, the lake does in fact exist, though not in the form observed by Stoddard. The mining engineer claimed he arrived at the precise location of the lost lake of gold only to discover it had been covered by a landslide, presumably during a collapse of the fractured and weakened headwall. Roberts found gold, and plenty of it, around the margins of the slide, but according to his report, the greater part of the lake was buried under hundreds of tons of rock.

Because of the rugged terrain and remote location, it is impossible to bring heavy earth-moving equipment into this area. Observations from other investigators who have found the lake have led to the conclusion that the only way to remove the covering of rock is to use dynamite to blast the large boulders into smaller chunks and employ human labor to clean out the basin. Such an undertaking could take months, if not years, and would require the efforts of several dozen men. In addition, the shock waves from a detonation of explosives may likely cause a second landslide.

The lake of gold effectively remains lost, though its existence is no longer in doubt. If the reports from those who claimed to have seen the gold are true, the largest accumulation of gold nuggets in North America may very well lie under several thousand tons of rock debris high in the Sierra Nevada Mountains.

Hobo Camp Gold

EARLY IN THE MORNING on October 11, 1894, outlaws Jack Brady and Sam Browning stopped an Overland Express train and robbed it of $50,000 in gold and silver coin. Inexperienced at such undertakings, the two outlaws quickly buried the money nearby and rode away, intending to return for it in the near future. Bad luck dogged their trail, however, and they were never able to retrieve their loot. Another man discovered the plunder quite by accident, helped himself to a portion of it, but then lost it again.

During the latter part of the nineteenth century, one of the major perils facing many railroad companies was train robbery. Successful bandits such as Frank and Jesse James, Sam Bass, and Butch Cassidy took hundreds of thousands of dollars' worth of coin and bullion from the railroads, most of which has never been recovered. These outlaws and their headline-grabbing robberies inspired numerous less talented but equally ambitious men who perceived an opportunity to gain some wealth with what they were convinced was a minimum of risk.

Brady and Sam Browning were small-time thieves who normally preyed on hapless travelers and prospectors in northern California.

As the Overland Express slowed during the climb up a steep grade east of Sacramento on this cool autumn morning in 1894 Jack Brady stationed himself in the middle of the tracks and waved the train to a halt. When Brady approached the locomotive, the engineer, a man named

Scott, leaned out of the cab to see what the problem was. At that moment, Sam Browning bounded out from behind a nearby clump of trees on the opposite side of the tracks, climbed into the cab, and leveled a shotgun at Scott and Bo Lincoln, the fireman. At gunpoint, Scott and Lincoln were led to the express car and told to order the messenger inside to open the door. When the messenger refused, Brady and Browning threatened to kill the two railroad employees. At this, the frightened messenger unlocked the door and slid it open.

Brady and Browning forced Scott and Lincoln inside the express car and commanded them to carry four canvas Wells Fargo sacks filled with gold and silver coins back to the engine. While Browning guarded Scott, Brady and the fireman uncoupled the engine from the rest of the train and the engineer was ordered to proceed.

The locomotive continued northeastward until it was a few miles outside of the small town of Washington when the outlaws told Scott to reduce the speed. As the huge engine slowed to a crawl, the outlaws threw the sacks of coins onto the ground and, after instructing Scott to continue on to Washington, jumped from the cab. As soon as the steam engine disappeared around a bend, the two men dragged the heavy sacks into the nearby trees and buried them.

The robbery had been carefully planned several days in advance by Brady and Browning. On the previous morning, the two outlaws had scouted the area and, deciding it would fit their needs nicely, excavated a hole in a thick grove of trees near the railroad tracks. This done, they hobbled two horses and left them to graze in a nearby meadow. Two hours later, they hopped a Sacramento-bound train, leaving it as it slowed down to enter the capital city. They spent the night in a ravine and the following morning prepared for the arrival of the outbound Overland Express.

After depositing the four sacks of money into the hole, they quickly covered it and retrieved the two horses. The two outlaws knew that when the robbery was reported, Wells Fargo agents would be swarming the countryside searching for two men with plenty of gold and silver to spend. The robbers decided to wait for several months for the pursuit and interest to lessen, at which time they intended to return to the cache and retrieve the loot.

Brady and Browning believed they had concocted a foolproof plan, but they overlooked one important element. In a small clearing about forty yards from where they buried the gold and silver coins was a hobo camp, a well known stop for the men who rode the freight trains from place to place in search of work. While Brady and Browning were sliding the canvas bags filled with gold and silver into the shallow excavation, a hobo named John Harmon was curled up behind a fallen log attempting to sleep off a severe headache he had acquired from the previous night's drinking. Conversation between the outlaws and the heavy clinking of the coins as they were dropped into the hole awakened Harmon. Peering over the top of the log, the sleepy-eyed tramp watched the two men cover the bags, all the while congratulating themselves on the success of the robbery.

When the train robbers rode away, Harmon crept out from behind his hiding place and approached the recently covered excavation. Scooping away the loose dirt, he pulled one of the heavy sacks out of the hole and noticed the words WELLS FARGO stenciled on the side. As his heart pounded faster, he unhooked the latches that held the bag closed and poured several coins out onto the ground.

Harmon sat next to the hole and the money for nearly an hour considering his good fortune. As his head cleared and the realization that he was rich began to encroach on his alcohol-dulled brain, he started formulating plans for his new-found wealth. He returned to the hobo camp a short distance back in the trees and waited quietly for about two hours as his contemporaries packed their gear and walked out to the railroad tracks where they climbed into an open box car pulled by a passing train. When everyone was gone, Harmon dug a hole near the edge of the camp. For the next hour and a half, he laboriously dragged the weighty sacks, one by one, from their original hiding place to the new one. Harmon removed $10,000 in gold and silver coins from the final sack and placed this money in his own pack. He covered the remaining $40,000 and then littered the area atop and around the hole with branches and other forest debris. When he was finished, the cache appeared exactly as the rest of the nearby forest. Hoisting his pack and bedroll, Harmon walked to the railroad tracks and awaited the next train bound for San Francisco.

After arriving at the Golden Gate City, Harmon rented a room, purchased some new clothes, and treated himself to the first shave and haircut he'd had in months. The next day, he opened a bank account into which he deposited most of his new money.

Claiming he had inherited a fortune from a wealthy relative who recently passed away in Europe, Harman began making the rounds of San Francisco high society and was often seen betting on the horses, gambling at popular night spots, and dining at the finest restaurants.

Harman also spent a great deal of money on women and he eventually became the constant companion of one Annabelle Vaughn who moved in with him. After returning from a short business trip to Sacramento, however, Harmon arrived at his hotel room only to discover that Vaughn had fled with a large amount of his cash. After checking his bank account and discovering he was running low on funds, Harmon decided he must return to the hobo camp soon and dig up another $10,000.

In the meantime, Jack Brady and Sam Browning had been identified as the robbers of the Overland Express train near Washington and law enforcement officers, accompanied by Wells Fargo agents, were searching the northern part of the state for the two outlaws. Browning was eventually killed in a hail of bullets as he attempted to rob another train on March 30, 1895. Brady was finally captured on July 25, 1895 and shortly thereafter confessed to the train robbery. After negotiating for a light prison sentence, Brady agreed to lead the lawmen to the money. No one was more surprised than the outlaw on discovering the $50,000 was missing! Brady was tried for his crime and sentenced to life in prison.

While investigating the site near the tracks pointed out by Brady, one of the Wells Fargo agents discovered the hobo camp nearby and questioned several of the occasional residents. The only information he gleaned was that one particular tramp named John Harmon seemed to have disappeared from the regular gatherings about the same time the train was robbed. The agent made a note of the circumstance and filed it with the rest of his report.

Several months later on February 7, 1896, a man sought an appointment with agents at the Wells Fargo office in San Francisco. During the subsequent meeting, the man stated he could offer some insight into the missing gold and silver coins if he were granted a reward. After a deal had been struck, the informer claimed that a friend of his spent a recent evening drinking with a man named John Harmon, and during the conversation that ensued, Harmon drunkenly bragged about digging up some train robbery loot near the railroad tracks not far from Washington. The next day, Wells Fargo detectives apprehended Harmon in a posh social club in downtown San Francisco.

Offering no resistance whatsoever, Harmon went along with the detectives and within the hour explained his role in digging up and reburying the train robbery loot. He did not believe he had done anything wrong and told the agents that $40,000 was still cached near the hobo camp.

Within the week, Harmon was taken by the agents to the camp to retrieve the remainder of the loot. Once they arrived at the site, however, the former tramp became disoriented and could not find the cache. With the help of the agents, he dug several holes but none of them yielded the money.

Harmon was subsequently charged with theft and sentenced to a few years in prison. When he was released, he returned to riding the freight cars and living in hobo camps for the next twenty years until his death.

Washington, California, is located in a picturesque setting in the Tahoe National Forest. Not far from this small town toward the southwest was once a popular spot where hoboes would gather, pool what food they possessed to make a "hobo stew," and sit by the campfire recalling their various adventures riding the rails of the growing country. The days of the hobo are long gone, and the old hobo camps of yesterday exist in only a few isolated places. The one near Washington fell into disuse almost one hundred years ago and it has since been reclaimed by the surrounding forest. The old site, which no one today can remember the exact location of, still contains four sacks of Wells Fargo gold and silver coins, a fortune that would be worth close to a million dollars today.

Lost Gold Coin Cache in Calvaras County

IN A LITTLE-KNOWN CANYON in the Mokelume Hills there exists a partially covered shaft of a small gold mine. Nearby, under a stout boulder, is a cache consisting of three metal boxes filled with gold coins. The owner of the mine and the cache was slain for his fortune, and the slayer met an untimely end before returning to the canyon to retrieve the treasure.

Slava Tyroff was born in Russia, migrated with his family to Europe when he was a child, and at eighteen years of age arrived on the shores of the United States in the late 1860s. Having heard stories of the productive gold fields in California, the young man traveled westward and finally arrived at San Francisco where he hoped to learn to speak English and grow wealthy finding gold.

Only after arriving in California did Tyroff learn that, while some prospecting for gold was still being undertaken, the glory days of the forty-niners were long past and most of the highly productive sites had been taken over by large companies. Tyroff learned that if an adventurous prospector cared to venture farther inland into regions heretofore unexplored, there might be a chance of finding gold.

The young Russian found a job sweeping floors and washing windows in a gambling hall for three dollars a week while he practiced his English and waited for opportunities to come his way.

Two years passed and finally one such opportunity presented itself. For nearly two months, Tyroff observed a man wearing overalls and well-worn boots who would come into the casino, try his luck at the tables, lose all of his money, and then depart with a dejected look. Though he squandered thousands of dollars at cards and dice, he always held a dollar back which he used to tip Tyroff.

One evening after losing big at the dice tables, the man stopped at the bar for a drink and struck up a conversation with the friendly Tyroff. He introduced himself as Harry Oversem and commented to the young Russian that he would leave in the morning for his gold mine and work hard all week to replace what he lost from gambling. Intrigued, Tyroff asked the man many questions about prospecting, mining, and gold.

Oversem, impressed by the young man's interest, offered him a job working at his mine. He told the young Russian that if he were willing to learn and contribute a lot of hard work, he would cut him in for one-half of the profits. Tyroff, eager for the opportunity to learn something about gold mining and the potential to make a lot of money, agreed to go into partnership with Oversem. That evening he resigned his job at the casino, and the next morning left with the miner.

For several days the two men traveled on horseback in a northeasterly direction from San Francisco, finally arriving at the small settlement of Mokelumne Hill. This town had a reputation for being wild and dangerous, and during the height of the gold rush days some twenty years earlier, it was not uncommon for three or four men to be shot or hung each day.

After picking up a few supplies and two burros he left at a livery stable, Oversem led Tyroff out of Mokelumne Hill, riding due east for about three miles. Near this point they crossed a wide mesa and traveled toward a range of hills incised by three major canyons. Entering the middle canyon, they climbed the steepening gradient for the remainder of the day before stopping about a quarter of a mile below the crest. Nearby was a small spring from which Oversem obtained water to make some coffee. As Tyroff got a small fire started, the miner stated that they would camp here for the night. Tyroff saw as he looked around that the site had been used as a camp many times in the past.

The following morning after a light breakfast, Oversem led Tyroff across the canyon floor and part way up the opposite side. Here, the miner removed a layer of pine boughs and revealed the opening to a deep shaft. This, he told Tyroff, was his gold mine.

Over the next few days Oversem taught Tyroff how to remove the ore from the crumbly quartz matrix, a thick vein of which ran deep into the mountain. Slowly, yet with impressive consistency, Tyroff dug the gold from the mine and placed it in small leather bags Oversem provided for the purpose. While Tyroff dug in the mine, the older man busied himself around the camp and sometimes rode to the mouth of the canyon to hunt deer.

After the first week, Tyroff had filled enough of the leather bags to load a burro. Oversem told the young man to guard the mine while he carried the gold to Mokelumne Hill to exchange it for coin. When Oversem returned, they would divide the money.

Two days later, Oversem returned and handed Tyroff a twenty dollar gold piece, telling him it was his share. How happy and excited was the Russian! Twenty dollars was so much more than he made in a week sweeping out the gambling casino. In fact, Tyroff now held in his hand more money than he ever possessed in his life. He couldn't wait for morning so that he could return to the mine and resume digging.

At the end of each week for the next six months, Oversem rode to Mokelumne Hill with one or two burros loaded down with gold, and each time he returned he would hand Tyroff a twenty dollar gold piece. On the evening following his return to the mine site, Oversem, on finishing dinner, would invariably rise, stretch, and inform young Tyroff that he was going for a short walk. If the Russian indicated he would like to go along, Oversem always discouraged him, telling him that he preferred to walk alone. Tyroff attached no significance to Oversem's evening stroll until one occasion when he decided to follow him.

In the mood for a short walk, Tyroff finished washing the dishes, and strolled down the canyon hoping to catch up with Oversem. A few minutes later, he saw the miner a short distance away wrestling with a stout rock, pushing it slightly to one side and exposing a small hole in the ground. Curious, Tyroff crept closer and watched from behind the bole of a large tree. Oversem's back was to the young Russian and Tyroff was unable to see what he was doing, but he heard the unmistakable sound of the clinking of gold coins into some kind of metal container. Tyroff counted each clink, reaching twenty-one before Oversem rose and replaced the large rock over the hole. As the man struggled with the rock, Tyroff silently returned to camp, pondering his discovery.

For several hours that night, Tyroff lay awake thinking about what he had witnessed earlier in the evening, and the more he thought the greater his anger. It gradually occurred to the young man that Oversem was cheating him, and he determined to do something about it.

Late that night while Oversem was sleeping soundly, Tyroff crawled out of his bedroll, laced up his boots, and walked down the canyon to the location where the miner had hidden the coins. Younger and stronger than Oversem, Tyroff had little difficulty pushing the heavy rock aside. This done, he examined the hole and found three metal boxes, each filled with twenty dollar gold pieces. Tyroff realized that Oversem had been cheating him out of his fair share all along. Furious at this deception, Tyroff returned to the camp.

On arriving at the campsite, Tyroff found Oversem sleeping soundly near the embers of the dead fire. Walking quietly over to the shaft, the Russian retrieved a sledgehammer and returned to the prone form. With one quick blow, Tyroff killed the sleeping man.

Once the deed was accomplished, Tyroff became frightened and decided to flee. He saddled Oversem's horse and, taking nothing from the camp save for some hard biscuits and beef jerky, he fled into the night. As he passed the rock which covered the huge fortune in gold coins, Tyroff decided he would return for it later. For the moment he only wished to place some distance between himself and the scene of the murder.

Eating as he rode and stopping only long enough to water himself and his horse, Tyroff finally reached the familiar environs of San Francisco. Before the day was over, he sold Oversem's horse and wandered down to the docks in search of work.

Tyroff went from ship to ship seeking employment. One evening as he spoke with a shifty-eyed, surly cargo handler, Tyroff was knocked unconscious from behind. The next morning he awoke aboard a schooner and discovered he had been abducted as a slave laborer.

It was nearly ten years later when Tyroff was finally able to return to San Francisco. For several days he walked the streets of the city familiarizing himself with the changed landscape. Tyroff decided he would spend a week here and then purchase a horse and burro, return to the canyon east of Mokelumne Hill, and retrieve the fortune in gold coins hidden beneath the large rock.

One evening, Tyroff entered a saloon and ordered a whiskey. As he stood at the bar nursing his drink, the bartender got into a loud argument with a customer at the far end of the bar. At the height of the argument the bartender, Charles Mason, grabbed the customer by the coat and began beating him across the head with the hilt of a large knife. Tyroff, noticing the customer was unarmed and much smaller than Mason, ran to his aid. When the Russian demanded that Mason release the smaller man, the bartender turned and struck him with the knife. The blade entered Tyroff's chest, slicing into a lung. Severely wounded, the Russian staggered backwards as Mason leaped over the bar and rushed him, slashing wildly with the now crimson blade. Once again the knife struck Tyroff, this time sinking deep into his abdomen. With some difficulty, he pulled a revolver from his belt and pumped three shots into Mason, killing him instantly. Only seconds after the dispute arose, the two combatants lay on the barroom floor, each in his own pool of blood.

A doctor was summoned, and within minutes, Michael Berlin entered the bar and surveyed the scene. It took the physician only a few seconds to pronounce Mason dead, but on examining Tyroff he discovered a weak pulse. Dr. Berlin realized he would have to act quickly if he were to save this man, so he ordered several stout tavern patrons to carry the Russian to his office where surgery was performed. The next morning, Tyroff awoke with a high fever and Berlin was not certain he would live. He informed the Russian his chances for survival were dim.

Later that evening when Berlin brought Tyroff some broth, the Russian, believing he was going to die, told the doctor about the gold buried in the canyon near Mokelumne Hill and provided directions to the location. He also confessed to killing Oversem. Berlin believed none of the Russian's tale of the buried coin cache and the murder, thinking it merely the product of a delirious mind.

A week later Tyroff, much to the surprise of the doctor and himself, recovered and, though still weak, was able to walk around on his own. He returned to the streets of San Francisco, intent on obtaining a horse and burro and returning to the canyon near Mokelumne Hill to retrieve the gold.

A week after leaving Berlin's office, Tyroff's body was found in San Francisco Bay. He had been shot in the head and Mason's brother was being held for investigation.

About three years later, Berlin decided to abandon California and return to Boston from where he had originally come. The stagecoach on which he traveled stopped overnight at Mokelumne Hill, and Berlin was reminded of the story told years earlier by Tyroff. Out of curiosity, Berlin asked the hotel clerk if he had ever heard of a man named Oversem and was told that he had been killed up in the mountains. When Berlin asked precisely where, the clerk provided directions that matched those given by Tyroff. Berlin decided to remain in the area and search for the gold.

Renting a horse, the physician spent the next two weeks exploring the mountains east of Mokelumne Hill. With little difficulty he located the canyon described by Tyroff, and a short time later found the site of Oversem's camp. Nearby, he located an old mine shaft, but it had been partially filled in by a landslide.

Walking down the canyon a short distance, Berlin looked around for a stout rock as described by the Russian. To his surprise and dismay, he found several that fit the description. Berlin spent the next three hours laboriously moving large rocks and searching the ground beneath them. He was unable to locate the cache of gold coins and eventually grew weary from his labors. A city-bred man unaccustomed to the rigors of wilderness travel and living, Berlin decided to abandon the canyon for the softer lifestyle of Boston. He rode out of the canyon, never to return.

Mokelumne Hills is located in Calaveras County about fifty miles northeast of Stockton. Since Dr. Berlin's exploration of the canyon described by Tyroff, only a few people have entered this region in search of Oversem's buried coins. This fortune, cached in three metal boxes and lying beneath a large rock, has never been found.

The Curse of the
Lost Cement Mine

TUCKED AWAY IN THE HIGH Sierra Nevada Mountains of California is a vein of dark conglomerate rock with the texture of hardened cement. Dotted thickly throughout this odd-looking deposit are peanut-sized nuggets of gold, enough to make several men incredibly wealthy. This strange formation has been found several times and gold has been mined from it, but unfortunately, each and every person who has been associated with this ore has died. The Lost Cement Mine, as the deposit has come to be called, is believed by many to have a curse on it, and normally adventurous prospectors and treasure hunters have refused to search for the rich mine for fear that they might be the next to die.

One day in 1857, two prospectors were examining an area just northeast of Mammoth Peak and south of Mono Lake when they discovered a horizontal outcrop of a reddish-colored conglomerate rock. Hacking away at the formation with a pick, one of the prospectors removed two nuggets he believed to be almost pure gold. After examining them, the second prospector declared the stones to be worthless. Convinced his analysis was correct, the first prospector continued to dig away at the formation for a period of three days, eventually filling a small sack with several fine nuggets. Around the campfire one evening, he told his companion that he intended to travel to San Francisco and have the gold submitted for assay. That night, after tucking his sack of gold nuggets into the foot of his bedroll before turning in, the prospector was seized by uncontrollable fits of coughing.

The next morning as he prepared his horse and pack mule for the long ride to San Francisco, the prospector was visibly weakened by the wracking coughs and the sleepless night. For the next two weeks he traveled through wind, rain, and some extremely rugged territory before finally arriving at the Golden Gate City. After leaving a sample of his gold at an assay office, the prospector found a physician to treat his cough, which had grown progressively worse.

His fears were realized when the doctor informed him he was suffering from tuberculosis and did not have very long to live. One evening as he lay on a cot in the doctor's office, the prospector told the physician, Dr. Randall, about his discovery of gold in the Sierra Nevada Mountains far to the east and showed him the assay report that verified it was indeed a very rich deposit. He gave Dr. Randall the sack of gold as payment for his services and drew a crude map showing him where the curious outcrop was located. The next day, the prospector died. To those who believed in curses, the Lost Cement Mine had claimed its first victim.

Intrigued at the prospect of finding gold in great quantity, Dr. Randall organized an expedition to travel to the Sierra Nevadas, find the gold deposit, and mine it. What Randall believed would be a single, simple trip turned into a seventeen year odyssey. Bad luck struck the physician at every turn. During the first expedition, the party was struck by a severe blizzard that lasted several days and forced the searchers to hole up in hastily constructed shelters of tree limbs. They were ill-prepared for the storm and three members of the group froze to death.

On subsequent trips to the Sierra Nevadas in search of the deposit, Randall discovered that the prospector's map was geographically inaccurate. Distances, directions, and landmarks were poorly recorded and the difficulty in following the map ultimately led to a great deal of confusion among the searchers.

Still, Randall refused to give up the search, and mounted

an expedition to locate the gold at least once every year for seventeen years. In 1874, A Randall-led party entered the Sierra Nevada Mountains and was preparing to cross a region known as the Cathedral Range when they were warned by settlers that the local Indians were attacking and slaughtering travelers. Randall and his group of twelve investors ignored the warnings and continued their trek. After crossing the Cathedral Range, the party was approaching Deadman's Pass when they were set upon by a large contingent of Indians. Poorly armed and unprepared for a battle with hostile forces, every member of the group was slaughtered within minutes.

In 1875, a prospector named Farnsworth had been panning for gold in the Owens River for several months when, while exploring a nearby canyon, he chanced upon an odd formation. Projecting slightly from the surrounding bedrock was a reddish-colored ledge that bore evidence of having been previously mined. Farnsworth later referred to the outcrop as having the appearance and texture of cement. On closer inspection, Farnsworth discovered the outcrop was filled with gold nuggets like, as he later said, "raisins in a cake." Farnsworth removed several of the nuggets and traveled to Sacramento where he looked up his old partner, Elias Creighton. Creighton returned to the Owens River with Farnsworth, and for several weeks the two men successfully dug gold from the cement-like conglomerate. When they had accumulated all their pack animals were able to carry, they set about dividing it up and making plans to transport it to San Francisco. That evening around the campfire, the two partners got into an argument over the split, and Farnsworth killed Creighton with a bullet to the head.

After burying Creighton, Farnsworth loaded all of the gold onto the pack animals and undertook the long trip to San Francisco. On the second day, as he led the animals along a narrow cliffside trail, one of the burros grew balky and refused to go any further. Carefully making his way to the rear of the small caravan on the precarious path,

Farnsworth was in the process of coaxing the recalcitrant burro along when the animal panicked and began kicking. Farnsworth was knocked off the trail and fell to his death into a canyon 300 feet below.

In 1877, a man named Kent came into the Owens River region of the Sierra Nevada Mountains. Kent was intent on panning some gold from the stream, but had heard tales of the so-called Lost Cement Mine and from time to time searched the canyons for it.

One afternoon while hunting for deer, Kent chanced upon an outcrop of red conglomerate. He would have passed the formation by had he not accidentally noticed some mining tools lying at the base of the outcrop. While examining one of the shovels, Kent happened to spot some color among the conglomerate deposit. Taking his knife and removing one of the gleaming stones, he was surprised to discover it was a gold nugget! As he examined the outcrop, Kent found evidence it had been previously worked and he concluded he finally found the Lost Cement Mine so widely discussed in this part of California.

Several months later, Kent arrived in San Francisco with three burro loads of gold. After converting the ore to cash, he banked most of his fortune and immediately sought out a tavern where he intended to celebrate. Well into the evening following several whiskeys, Kent began complaining of chest pains. Believing the discomfort would soon go away he continued to drink with several new-found friends. When he could stand the pain no longer, Kent excused himself, saying he needed to go to his room, but before he reached the front door of the tavern he collapsed and died from a heart attack.

Those who have researched the Lost Cement Mine over the years claim that Kent was the last known victim of the alleged curse associated with the gold. According to the investigators, over two dozen men are believed to have died as a result of their connection to this curious outcrop located in the Sierra Nevada Mountains.

Southern California

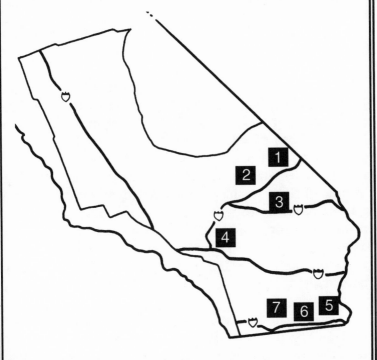

1. Lost Underground River of Gold
2. Golden Stones of the Avawatz Mountains
3. Dutch Oven Mine
4. G.C. Lee Mine
5. Pothole Gold
6. Hill of Black Gold
7. Lost Ship

The Lost Underground River of Gold

Long before white settlers arrived in the perceived promised-
land of California, the regional Indians spoke amongst themselves about the existence of an underground river, the
banks and bed of which were allegedly replete with pure
gold nuggets. When settlers and gold-seekers made their way
to the Golden State, many of them heard these stories but
attributed them to the imaginative tribal mythology and
folklore of the heathen inhabitants. Even today, a few older
members of some of the California tribes speak guardedly
about this lost river of gold that flows beneath the sands and
rocks of the Mojave Desert, but for the most part they
remain silent.

The Indians were not always secretive about the river of
gold. During the early 1920s, two Mojave Indians regularly
removed gold from the banks of this subterranean river, gold
which they carried to the nearest settlements to trade for
food and ammunition. Most people assumed the Mojaves
found the gold at some isolated surface location out in the
desert, but a prospector named Earl Dorr discovered otherwise. After befriending the two Indians, Dorr was presented
with a map to the underground stream and the gold, a map
that started Earl Dorr toward a promising yet troubled quest.

Earl Dorr was one of many old-time prospectors who
could still be seen wandering in and around the Mojave
Desert during the first two decades of the twentieth century.
Leading his supplies-laden burro, Dorr was always welcome
at the many prospector and hobo camps found scattered

throughout the southern California desert. During his visits to some of these camps, Dorr heard the oft-repeated tale of a mysterious cave supposedly located high in a local mountain range, a cave which followed a twisting and dangerous route far down into the mountain and below, finally arriving at the shores of the legendary river. Dorr considered the tale mere Indian superstition and dismissed it out of hand until one fateful day when he encountered two Mojave Indians in the desert.

Dorr and the Indians arrived simultaneously but from different directions at a well-known spring in the foothills of the Bristol Mountains. The spring afforded plenty of water and the location was a popular stop adjacent to a heavily traveled desert trail. The three men shared what food they had and settled into relaxed conversation around the evening fire. When Dorr told the two Indians he was prospecting for gold, they pulled out a small leather bag and spilled the contents onto a blanket spread out in front of the bright blaze. Dorr stared in amazement at the quantity of gold nuggets lying before him. Picking one up and examining it, he found himself quite impressed with the quality of the ore, some of the finest he had ever seen.

It was a general rule among the old-time prospectors that one never inquired about the location of another's claim, therefore as Dorr returned the glistening nugget to the pile before him, he smilingly thanked the Indians for allowing him to look at their gold and congratulated them on their success. Dorr was taken by complete surprise, however, when one of the Indians asked him if he would like to go to where the gold came from and see it for himself. When the prospector told them he certainly would, they drew a crude map on a piece of canvas and gave it to him. The next morning the Indians continued westward toward Barstow, and Dorr, carrying the map in his shirt pocket, led his burro toward the east and a mountain the Indians called Kokoweef

Because of the extremely crude imagery portrayed on

the map and the rugged environment around Kokoweef Mountain, Dorr had a difficult time locating the entrance to the cave. For three days he hiked and climbed along the side of the mountain until one evening he spotted a tiny crack in the rock. On investigating, he discovered it was the cave of which the Indians had spoken.

The next morning Dorr, armed with several grass torches, entered the opening. After wriggling his way for about twenty yards along the narrow passage, the cavern opened into a large chamber with a ceiling so high the flickering torches were unable to illuminate it. At the end of the chamber, the passageway slanted downward at an angle that required a rope. Not having one, the prospector returned to his camp and made preparations to explore the cave the following morning.

Just after sunup, Dorr entered the mouth of the cave once again carrying torches and rope. He lowered himself approximately one hundred feet down the angled passageway which opened into another chamber, this one much smaller than the first. Here, Dorr rested for several minutes, and casually burned his name on one of the walls with a torch.

At the end of this chamber was another slanting passageway, but not so steep as the first so it did not require a rope. At the end was yet another chamber with a tubular passageway on one side. Following this, Dorr came upon still another chamber and another passageway, this one so low and narrow it had to be negotiated on hands and knees. As he explored the many chambers and passageways of the cavern, Dorr noted that he was climbing and crawling downward and estimated he had descended to about the level of the surrounding plain.

After crawling for about an hour, Dorr entered another huge chamber which he later described as being large enough to contain a twenty story building, with no walls in sight. In the center of the chamber and running along its length was a deep canyon, and though Dorr was unable to see the bottom of it, he could hear the sound of water coursing along a stream far below.

The prospector estimated he had crawled, climbed, and hiked several miles inside the cavern in search of a route to the floor of the canyon. Finally, he discovered a narrow trail which led downward, and after following a series of switchbacks, he found himself walking on dark, almost black sand. Squatting at the edge of the underground river, he sifted some of the sand through his fingers and marveled at the quantity of gold flakes and nuggets that reflected the light of his torch. Deftly, Dorr picked several of the larger nuggets from the palmful of sand and placed them in a shirt pocket. In another pocket he placed a handful of the sand.

Dorr watched the clear waters of a wide underground stream flowing past and realized he was probably the first white man to ever witness this legendary river. The light of his torch was unable to penetrate the darkness enough to see the opposite bank. Walking up and down the edge of the stream for several hundred yards, he found gold everywhere he looked. Dorr concluded a limitless fortune lay at his feet, and he began to concoct a plan to bring most of it to the surface.

Tired and hungry as a result of his efforts, Dorr finally decided to return to his camp. Following an exhaustive climb back out, he exited the narrow opening and was greeted by a nearly full moon and a sky filled with bright stars. Dorr had been in the cave nearly eighteen hours!

During the following months, Dorr attempted to secure investments to finance his new gold mining venture, but each person to whom he related his tale thought him crazy. In the meantime, he filed a claim on the area. Finally in 1927, using his own limited funds, Dorr hired a mining engineer and took him into the cave. Weeks later, the engineer filed a report which essentially confirmed everything Dorr claimed.

Still unable to obtain financing, Dorr borrowed some money and purchased a great deal of mining equipment and supplies at Barstow. Loading several burros with his new equipment, he made the long trip out to Kokoweef Peak and Crystal Cave, as he had come to call the cavern.

On the way to the cave, Dorr stopped at one of the old prospector encampments and visited with some friends for a while. He told them about the cave and, though his friends did not believe him, they all wished him success. Dorr told them he would return in about three or four days and show them the kind of gold that could be taken from the underground river. The following morning, Dorr loaded dynamite, ropes, lanterns, food, and shovels onto his pack animals and departed.

After a week had gone by and Dorr did not return, his friends grew worried and decided to search for him. They easily located his camp near the base of Kokoweef Mountain, and several hours later found the entrance to the cave. Inside the cavern, they found where their friend had cached some of his recent purchases. One of the men discovered a rope ladder in the slanting shaft, and after securing two of the lanterns among Dorr's supplies, they all cautiously descended.

The group of Dorr's friends had reached the final small chamber when they encountered the miner exiting the small passageway on his hands and knees, dragging behind him a detonating device and a length of wire. When Dorr saw his friends, he misinterpreted their interest in his well-being and began to accuse them of trying to steal his gold. He attacked them, striking with his fists and screaming as though half-crazed. As the well-intentioned intruders attempted to subdue the violent Dorr, the detonating device was accidentally activated and an explosion followed deep in the shaft from which Dorr recently crawled. Seconds later, dust from the blast came pouring out of the narrow passageway and filled the chamber, forcing the men to seek safety at higher levels. Dragging the subdued Dorr behind them, they headed back toward the entrance.

The explosion shattered the walls and ceiling of the only passageway leading to the canyon and the underground river of gold. Rock and debris collapsed and filled the tunnel, effectively closing it and preventing access to the riches Dorr claimed lay on the other side. The task now facing the miner was to clear the tunnel of debris, a job that would require the labor of several men over a long period of time. Once again, Dorr decided to try to attract some investors in the hope of funding the excavation process.

Dorr was unable to raise the money during the next several years. In addition, the claim he had filed earlier was in dispute and he learned it did not include the entrance to the cavern. When Dorr went to refile, he discovered someone else had already claimed this section.

Though discouraged and disappointed, Dorr refused to give up. In 1934, he had a lawyer draw up an affadavit attesting to the discovery of gold in the sands of the underground river. For six years, he tried to use this affadavit to secure financing but had no luck. The statement was eventually published in the November 1940 issue of the *California Mining Journal*, a publication serving commercial miners and mining companies:

> To Whom It May Concern:
> This is to certify that there are located in San Bernadino County, California, certain caverns. These caverns are about 250 miles from Los Angeles, California. Traveling over state highways by automobile, the caverns can be reached in a few hours.
> Accompanied by a mining engineer, I visited the caverns in the month of May, 1927. We entered them and spent four days exploring them for a distance of between eight and nine miles. We carried with us altimeters and pedometers, to measure the distance
> we traveled, and had an instrument to take

measurements of distance by triangulation, together with such other instruments convenient and necessary to make observations and estimations.

Our examinations revealed the following facts, viz:

1. From the mouth of the cavern we descended about 2,000 feet. There, we found a canyon which, on our altimeter, measured about 3,000 to 3,500 feet deep. We found the caverns to be divided into many chambers, filled and embellished with the usual stalactites and stalagmites, besides many grotesque and fantastic wonders that make the caverns one of the marvels of the world.

2. On the floor of the canyon there is a flowing river which by careful examination and measurement (by triangulation) we estimated to be about 300 feet wide, and with considerable depth. The river rises and falls with the tides of the sea—at high tide being approximately 300 feet wide, and at low tide, approximately ten feet wide and four feet deep.

3. When the tide is out there is exposed on both sides of the river from 100 to 150 feet of black sand which is very rich in gold value. The sands are from four to eleven feet deep. This means there are about 300 to 350 feet of rich gold bearing placer sand which averages eight feet in depth. We explored the canyon sands a distance of eight miles, finding little variation in the depth and width of the sands.

4. I am a practical miner of many years of experience and I own valuable mining properties nearby which I am willing to pledge and put up as security to guarantee that the statements herein are true.

5. My purpose in exploring the caverns was to study the mineralogy in order to ascertain the mineral possibilities and the actualities of the caves, making such examination in person with my mining engineer necessary to determine by expert examination the character and quantity of mineral values of the caverns, rocks and sands.

6. I carried out about 10 pounds of the black sand and 'panned' it, receiving more than $7 in gold. I sold it to a gold buyer who offered me the rate of $18 per ounce. Two and one-half pounds of this black sand I sent to John Herman, assayer, whose assay certificates show a value of $2145.47 per yard, with gold at $20.67 per ounce.

7. From engineering measurements and observations we made, I estimate that it would require a tunnel about 350 feet long to penetrate to the caverns, 1000 feet or more below the present entrance, which are some three miles distant from my property.

8. I make no estimate of even the approximate tonnage of the black sand, but some estimate of the cubical contents may be made for more than eight miles and the minimum depth is never less than three feet. They are of varying depths— what their maximum depth may be we do not know.

Sworn to by: E.P. Dorr
309 Adena Street
Pasadena, California
November 16, 1934.

Dorr's affadavit eventually came to the notice of a Los Angeles entrepreneur named Herman Wallace. Wallace formed the Crystal Cave Mining Company and attracted several investors with the possibilities of removing millions of dollars worth of gold ore from the black sands of the underground river.

After several weeks of examining the mountain, an engineering team found a small cave on the southwestern slope of Kokoweef Mountain. From this cave, they deduced, a tunnel could be excavated to link up with Crystal Cave.

Tons of mining equipment were brought to the site and the excavation began. As the digging proceeded and the shaft penetrated deeper and deeper into the mountainside, the air inside the tunnel grew stale and close and became a serious problem for the miners—several had to be carried out after collapsing from lack of oxygen. Eventually, the workers refused to enter the shaft and Wallace began to search for a new approach to penetrate Crystal Cave. Soon another small cave was found nearby and plans were being made to attempt to dig a tunnel when a high grade of zinc ore was discovered.

During this time, zinc was in great demand across the nation by manufacturers of automobile tires and automotive parts. With the recent outbreak of World War I, the use of zinc increased dramatically and Herman, realizing a fortune could be made from this large body of ore located near the surface, abandoned all efforts to enter Crystal Cave and began mining zinc. Dorr was summarily dismissed and the mining company no longer expressed any interest in retrieving the gold.

On his own, Dorr continued excavating the tunnel already begun in the first small cave but eventually gave up. Nearly penniless, he lacked the funds to retain an engineer to direct his activities. Finally, he was forced to abandon the project.

Dorr made several attempts during the next twelve years to generate some interest among potential investors to go after the gold of the underground river, but by now he had attained the reputation of a failure and no one cared to become involved in his scheme. Dorr passed away in 1957, and to the last he maintained his belief in the existence of a fortune in gold in the sands of the underground river.

* * *

Throughout the years many have expressed doubts about the existence of a lost underground river and accompanying gold-filled sands. Several professional geologists have offered the opinion that such a river and gold deposit were pure impossibilities. Many who knew Dorr personally claimed they never actually believed his fantastic tale.

In 1948, a team of experienced cave explorers decided to investigate Crystal Cave. The group was led by Dr. William R. Halliday, a member of the National Speleological society.

The group, a total of 34 members, entered the narrow opening and explored the chambers and passageways, finally arriving at the tunnel Dorr accidentally blasted shut. Unable to proceed, they returned to the surface. Along the way they discovered Dorr's name inscribed in smoke on a wall.

When the party returned to their home base in Pasadena, Halliday was interviewed by the local newspaper. In response to a reporter's question, the speleologist stated that there was every possibility that a large river existed several hundred feet below the last level they penetrated in the cave. He claimed he found a great deal of evidence of a major fault running through the area and hypothesized that the stream flowed along this fracture.

* * *

Dorr's tunnel has never been reopened. Several teams of miners and mining engineers have investigated the collapsed shaft deep in the cave and in each case came away convinced such an attempt would be extremely dangerous. Tons of rubble completely filled the passageway and it was also observed that the blast weakened the layer of rock which comprised the immediate roof of the chamber and that it exhibits a great potential for collapse.

There is no possibility of bringing heavy digging equipment to this site to penetrate the passageway. The only alternative, according to the investigators, is to use human labor, but they cautioned that the shaft is so small and narrow it would make excavation difficult as well as hazardous.

Some of the older Indians who live in this area claim they know of another entrance to the underground river of gold, but they refuse to reveal the location, maintaining it is a tribal secret.

In the meantime, one of the richest gold deposits in North America lies intact and untouched deep underground beneath a remote mountain in the Mojave Desert.

Golden Stones of the Avawatz Mountains

THE AVAWATZ MOUNTAINS are a little known range located just south of Death Valley, their southern edge visible from the old emigrant trail that bisected this arid region between Las Vegas to San Bernadino. While some prospecting and mining activity has taken place in this range, the Avawatz Mountains have never been regarded as a very productive area. Still, rumors of great deposits of gold here continued to bring hopeful miners to the area. With the exception of a few small claims that paid rather poorly, these mountains have seen relatively little activity. But somewhere in this range, according to a traveler who claimed to have seen it, lies a hill literally covered with brownish-colored rocks composed of almost pure gold.

Around 1850, Mormon leader Brigham Young charged a number of his followers to travel to southwestern California to found the city of San Bernadino and colonize the area. A wagon train carrying the colonizers departed Salt Lake City and made the long, arduous journey through southern Utah, the length of Nevada, and finally across the scorching Mojave desert to the more fertile highlands near the San Gabriel Mountains.

Of the Mormons who remained in Utah, one desperately missed his friends who had gone to California and he longed to join them. Finally, he sold his ranch and livestock, outfitted himself with a sturdy wagon, supplies, and two good mules, and set out alone for the Golden State. After several weeks of difficult travel and inclement weather, he arrived at Vegas Ranch (now Las Vegas) where he and his mules remained for some much-needed rest.

Several days later, the Mormon struck out on the emigrant trail taken earlier by his friends and relatives. Sudden desert thunderstorms accompanied by flash floods and high winds had shifted tons of sand obliterating the poorly marked trail. As a result, the Mormon became lost and wandered into the Avawatz Mountains.

For days, the Mormon coaxed his mules across deep ravines and over sharp ridges. Water was scarce and he was running low on food by the time he found himself descending the rolling, rock-studded western slope of the range.

Weakened from a meager diet of desert vegetation, the mules grew balky and at times refused to continue. It was only after constantly lashing the poor beasts that the Mormon was able to get them to pull the wagon at all. Finally, near the limit of their endurance, the mules halted during a climb up a low hill and refused to proceed any further. When even whipping brought no response from the animals, the Mormon got out of the wagon and tried to lead them up the incline, but they wouldn't budge. Finally, in a fit of frustration and desperation, he grabbed a handful of rocks and began pelting the hindquarters of the mules as hard as he could. The animals responded by slowly and laboriously climbing the hill. Encouraged, the Mormon filled his pockets with several more of the heavy, dark-colored stones.

A short time later, the Mormon came to a spring where he and the animals rested for three days. Refreshed and recovered from the long ordeal in the Avawatz Mountains, he continued on to San Bernadino, finally arriving at the growing community several days later.

After making arrangements to stay with friends, the Mormon decided he needed to purchase a new suit of clothes, his only pants, shirt, and jacket having gotten ripped in several places during the long journey. After making the purchase, the frugal Mormon left his old clothes with a seamstress at a local tailor shop to be mended. While arranging the ragged clothes for repairing, the seamstress removed several stones from the pockets and left them in a pile near her table. Later in the day, the proprietor of the tailor shop walked by the stones and, out of curiosity, picked one up. Surprised at the unexpected weight of the stone, he scraped away a layer of the dark encrustation that covered it and was astounded to discover he was holding a piece of pure gold! After examining each of the remaining stones and finding all of them to be gold, he sent word for the Mormon to come to his shop immediately.

When the Mormon arrived, the proprietor led him into his office, showed him the small pile of stones now stacked neatly on his desk, and asked him if he knew what they were. The Mormon replied that they were merely stones he carried along to pitch at his mules to get them to move. When the proprietor told the Mormon they were large gold nuggets, the immigrant could scarcely believe it and told him of the low hill near the Avawatz Mountains that was almost completely covered with such rocks. He told the proprietor that he was certain he could relocate the hill. Together, the two men took the stones to the nearest assay office, had them evaluated, and learned that they were indeed almost pure gold.

After making preparations and purchasing supplies, the Mormon and the tailor left San Bernadino for the Avawatz Mountains. About two weeks later they arrived at the spring where the Mormon camped after coming out of the range. Certain he could make his way back to the gold-littered hill, the Mormon led the way into the mountains. Time and again they encountered low hills covered with dark-colored rocks, but they never found gold.

After nearly three months of searching, the two men finally ran out of supplies and were forced to return to San

Bernadino. The proprietor of the tailor shop gave up all hope of the Mormon ever relocating the rich hill and returned to his occupation. The Mormon, still certain he could find the gold, made several more trips into the Avawatz Mountains, but to no avail.

Around 1907, the story of the low gold-covered hill was well known to Californians and fortune seekers crisscrossed the Avawatz Mountains and associated foothills by the hundreds in search of it. There were several claims made about discovery of large amounts of gold, but none held up under investigation.

There are dozens of researchers today who are convinced that the story of the low hill covered with brownish-colored gold rocks is true, but attempts to locate it have become more complicated now that this area is now located within the boundary of the Fort Irwin Military Reservation, a fenced and carefully guarded expanse of land closed to the public.

The Lost Dutch Oven Mine

SOMEWHERE DEEP IN THE CLIPPER MOUNTAINS in the southeastern part of the state lies one of the most mysterious and puzzling lost mines in the history of California. The mystery is twofold: The actual site of this apparently very rich deposit has been seen by at least two people, but it has never been relocated; the original miner or miners seemed to have suddenly disappeared from the site after having established a semi-permanent camp, leaving no trace whatsoever. When they left, they left an expertly excavated shaft containing several seams of rich gold ore and a large cast iron dutch oven completely filled with almost pure gold nuggets.

During the 1890s, young Tom Schoffield was hired to provide water for the Santa Fe Railroad when the train stopped at Danby, a small settlement located along the tracks in eastern San Bernadino County. Crossing the arid landscape between Needles and Barstow, the train stopped at several locations to take on needed water, and the job of procuring this precious commodity was considered very important. Tom Schoffield took his job quite seriously and was constantly on the lookout for auxiliary water sources. One day while based at Danby, Schoffield hiked into the nearby Clipper Mountains searching for freshwater springs that he might be able to tap as a dependable water source. While exploring around the foothills, he encountered a small spring and marked its location on the chart he carried for that purpose. Just as he was about to leave the area, Schoffield noticed an old, dim, and partially overgrown trail leading away from the spring and up into an adjacent, steep-walled canyon. Schoffield was under the impression that this mountain range had never been hunted, occupied or even explored, so out of curiosity he started to follow the trail, a decision that eventually led him to the most amazing adventure of his life.

The narrow, rock-strewn trail wound up the canyon, across a narrow ridge, down yet another canyon, and across a second ridge. Soon tiring of following a path that appeared to go no place in particular, Schoffield was about to turn back when he noticed that, a short distance ahead and downslope, it passed through a narrow space in the rocks of a canyon, a space barely wide enough to allow the passage of a man. Wondering what might lie on the other side of the pass, Schoffield squeezed through the restricted opening and, as he came out the other side, he saw that the path led toward two large boulders. Making his way past the first, he was surprised to come upon an abandoned camp bearing all the indications of having been occupied by miners. Nearby was a tent, partially torn and shredded by exposure to the constant winds that blew in the canyon. Pieces of torn canvas flapped in the breeze, but intact within was a pallet made from pine boughs and two blankets. Scattered about the ground were cooking gear, a pair of worn-out boots, and several mining tools including hammers, drills, and ore buckets. Lying near a ring of stones that encircled a fire pit was a large cast iron dutch oven, the lid fitted precisely onto the top. Walking past the oven, Schoffield encountered a pile of old railroad ties that had been cut up to serve as mine timber. The camp had the look of having been deserted for several weeks, and from the way goods and supplies were left lying about, the former occupants apparently left in a hurry.

Schoffield picked up the trail on the other side of the camp and followed it for another forty yards when he came to a deep, vertical mine shaft. The shaft extended about eighty feet into the granite of the canyon floor and appeared to follow a series of parallel veins of gold-filled blue-tinted quartz. The deeper the shaft, the wider the veins, indicating the richest part of the mine had yet to be excavated.

Schoffield examined the mine and explored around the area until dusk. Not wanting to hike the long distance back to Danby in the dark, he opted to camp for the night in the raggedy old tent.

After spending a quiet night sleeping soundly, Schoffield was awake at dawn and back at the shaft. Poking through the large pile of talus lying adjacent to the opening, he found several pieces of rough quartz filled with gold. Apparently whoever worked the mine brought the rock to the surface and, after accumulating a large quantity of it, proceeded to remove the gold from the matrix. Most of the rock in the talus pile still contained impressive amounts of ore. Schoffield selected several pounds of gold-filled quartz and placed it in his pockets.

Since Schoffield hadn't eaten in approximately eighteen hours, he was beginning to feel the pangs of hunger. Wondering if some canned goods might be found among the debris of the abandoned camp, he began poking around in search of something to eat. Finding nothing, he wandered over to the large dutch oven, idly lifted the lid and, to his great surprise, discovered the inside was filled with gold ore!

Emptying his pockets of the rock he gathered at the mine, Schoffield refilled them with the almost pure gold from the oven. His pants were so heavy from the gold that it was difficult to walk. As he started down the trail, Schoffield had thoughts of resigning his job as soon as he returned to Danby, procuring a couple of burros and some supplies, and returning to this area to mine his fortune from the ground.

After stopping at Danby long enough to leave a message informing his employers that he had quit, Schoffield continued on to Los Angeles where he had his gold assayed and made preparations to return to the Clipper Mountains.

About a month later, young Tom Schoffield returned to

Danby. Well-supplied and eager, he led his burros along the foothills of the range in search of the tiny spring near which he initially had found the trail that led to the gold mine. At the end of the first day, Schoffield had not found the water source and was growing worried. He was beginning to wonder if he was even in the correct area. Two more days passed, and still the spring could not be found. Schoffield was mentally cursing himself for not making a map of the area at the time of his discovery. When he was nearly to the point of panic, he finally located the spring late in the afternoon of the fourth day of searching.

After filling his canteens, Schoffield led his burros up the old trail and into the canyon. As he walked along, Schoffield had a feeling there was something different about the area. After pondering on it for several moments he finally realized that flash floods from recent rainstorms had washed away parts of the already dim and overgrown trail. Time and again he lost the path and would often have to tie his burros to a tree while he circled the area until he found it again.

Somewhere between the first and second ridge, Schoffield got lost and spent nearly three more days wandering around until he picked up the trail. Another two days passed and during that period he lost the trail several more times. Though he tried for nearly a week, he could never find it. Discouraged, he returned to Danby.

For the next fifty years, Tom Schoffield searched throughout the Clipper Mountains for what he referred to as the Lost Dutch Oven Mine. To the many searchers and researchers who visited with this gentle, sincere man over the years, Schoffield was always regarded as honest and completely convinced of the existence of this rich mine. But Tom Schoffield, who devoted the remainder of his life to walking and riding hundreds of miles in the Clipper Mountains range in search of the elusive shaft he accidentally found one day, was destined never to relocate it.

The Lost George C. Lee Mine

SOMEWHERE IN SAN BERNADINO COUNTY just a few miles east of the town of Lucerne Valley lies a lost, and apparently immensely rich, silver mine. This mine, by all accounts very productive, was discovered and operated by George C. Lee. Lee was brutally murdered and the circumstances surrounding his death remain one of California's most baffling mysteries, one that involves incredible wealth, broken promises, and the participation of a man who would eventually become governor of California.

George C. Lee arrived in California around 1851. Originally from New Jersey, he was lured to the west by tales of gold mining opportunities. Carrying just a simple rucksack with his few belongings and a head full of dreams, Lee believed he would someday strike it rich.

During the next few years Lee had some successes: He earned a good living from ore he extracted from a small mine located near the town of Volcano, and he apparently profited from the operation of a silver mine near Austin, Nevada. Around 1878, Lee eventually returned to California and settled in San Bernadino. There he married a lovely Indian woman and the two established a home in town while Lee roamed the surrounding hills in search of color.

After a few weeks of prospecting, Lee discovered a vein of silver over fifty miles to the north near Barstow, and before long he was hauling several sacks of ore into town every two or three weeks.

Lee was not a man given to quiet or humility. In the

San Bernadino taverns, the tall, large-boned, white-bearded, and generally unkempt prospector drank copiously, loudly boasting of his mining successes and crowing about his imagined importance. Lee's manner was often abrasive and insulting, and few men cared to share drinks with him. According to reports, Lee expressed little or no concern for anyone save his wife.

Only one man in San Bernadino showed any interest whatsoever in Lee. He was a local businessman and politician named Robert W. Waterman. Waterman held an interest in several area mines, and was well-respected in San Bernadino, an educated man of some breeding and stature. Most wondered why Waterman bothered to associate with the coarse and filthy Lee, but the scheming politician perceived certain opportunities associated with the bragging miner, opportunities that he believed could lead to the acquisition of substantial wealth.

After Lee announced the recent discovery of his rich silver mine and began spending heavily in the saloons, Waterman sought several audiences with him, and soon the two were often seen involved in deep discussions around a table, Waterman always providing an ample supply of whiskey.

Several weeks passed, and Lee announced he had gone into partnership with Waterman. Together, he claimed, the two would soon become very rich from the productive silver mine, which they called the Pencil Lead Mine. The prospector and the politician shook hands on the bargain, and Waterman promised to have the necessary papers prepared over the next few days.

About a week following the verbal agreement, Waterman asked to be taken to see the mine before he paid for his half-interest. The next morning the two partners, accompanied by three of Waterman's employees, rode into the Red Mountains near Barstow. Waterman gathered some samples of ore and returned to San Bernadino where he had them assayed. He was surprised and pleased to discover the ore was considerably richer than even Lee believed.

The next day, Waterman checked on the claim and discovered Lee had apparently never filed one! Many believed that Lee, eager to begin drinking at the first tavern he came to, simply forgot to file a claim on his mine. Without saying anything to Lee, Waterman filed the claim in his own name.

Two weeks later Lee returned from the mine leading four mules loaded down with ore. While the silver was being converted to cash, Lee, like Waterman several days earlier, discovered it was worth much more than he originally believed.

Unable to hold his tongue, Lee walked into a saloon, bragged about his good fortune, and stated to all in attendance that because of the recent assay he had decided not to go into partnership with Waterman after all. It wasn't long before Waterman learned of Lee's intentions.

Several weeks later, Lee arrived at his mine with a string of pack mules and enough supplies to last nearly a month. As he rode up to the diggings he was surprised to be greeted by Waterman's three employees, each of whom was pointing a rifle at the miner. The men informed Lee that Waterman possessed the claim on the mine and told him that he was trespassing. Furious, Lee returned to San Bernadino and discovered that the claim was in fact legally registered in Waterman's name.

For weeks Lee blustered and threatened in front of several witnesses that he intended to kill Waterman, but few paid much attention to the prospector and most believed he got what he deserved.

Months passed, and Lee's bank account was nearly depleted. Once again he took to the hills in search of a new vein of ore. Nearly a year later, the miner located another rich vein of silver near a place called Old Woman Springs near the town of Victorville. Not trusting to file his claim in San Bernadino, Lee traveled to Los Angeles and sought the advice of one of the few men he could claim as a friend.

Sam Stewart was an assayer who informed Lee that his discovery was extremely rich, but because it was located in San Bernadino County, the claim had to be filed at the county seat. Believing that Waterman would somehow cheat him out of his new discovery, Lee decided not to file and to continue to work at his claim in secret. Unfortunately, Lee was unable to refrain from his usual bragging tendencies, and soon everyone in San Bernadino knew of the existence of the secret mine.

During the next few months of clandestine travel to his mine and long, solitary hours of excruciating labor in the ever-lengthening shaft, Lee became a rich man. His bank account swelled and his standard of living rose considerably. One morning before departing to work at his mine, Lee hired a team of architects to design a fine new home for himself and his wife.

As Lee rode out of town, several observers noticed that he was followed by two horsemen. One citizen identified the men as Regis Brown and Hans Hoffman, both employees of Waterman. It was the last time anyone saw George C. Lee alive.

What happened next has been reconstructed from accounts provided by notes left by the county sheriff, court records, and newspaper reports.

As Lee approached the location of his secret mine in the area near Old Woman Springs, he discovered he was being followed. From a vantage point he could discern the two riders in the distance and cursed himself for being so careless. On previous occasions he had been tailed after leaving town but had always been successful in eluding his trackers. This time, thought Lee, the men behind were dangerously close to the mine. Lee decided to hide in a grove of willows that were nourished by the clear waters of the spring and await the approach of the two men. As Brown and Hoffman rode up to the spring, Lee suddenly stepped out from behind a tree and invited the two surprised men to dismount and talk.

Hoffman, known to drink as much as Lee, pulled a bottle of whiskey from his saddlebags and soon the three were passing the liquor back and forth as they parleyed.

Lee eventually told the two newcomers he believed they were trying to locate his secret mine for Waterman. By this time, all three of the men were quite drunk. Lee became loud and belligerent, and told Brown and Hoffman that he intended to kill Waterman the next time he was in town. In fact, he said, he thought he might as well kill both of them while they were here. Taking Lee's threat seriously, Hoffman excused himself on the pretense of needing to see to his horse. A few minutes later, as Lee was deep in conversation with Brown, Hoffman crept up behind the miner and bashed in the back of his skull with a huge rock, killing him instantly.

Two days later, a pair of travelers discovered Lee's body and reported it to San Bernadino County Sheriff John Burkhart. Within two days, Brown and Hoffman were arrested as suspects in Lee's murder. Brown was eventually released, and Waterman hired several attorneys to defend Hoffman who was officially charged with the murder. During the trial, which lasted six months, Waterman, based on information provided by Brown and Hoffman, traveled to the Old Woman Springs and undertook a search for Lee's rich mine. Though he spent several days hunting for some sign of the mine, he never found it.

When he was not searching for Lee's secret silver mine, Waterman attended Hoffman's trial proceedings. Eventually, a mistrial was declared and a second trial was scheduled. Following another six weeks of argument, the jury was deadlocked and no decision was rendered. While out on bail, Hoffman mysteriously disappeared and was never seen again.

For the next several years, Waterman continued to search for Lee's lost silver mine. In the meantime, Lee's widow sued the businessman for conspiracy in her husband's death and received a staggering $300,000. Waterman was also sued by his brother, by then a one-third partner in the Pencil Lead Mine. The brother contended he was cheated out of a half-million dollars in profits gleaned from the mine. Though the plaintiff died during the trial, Waterman was found guilty and ordered to pay a huge sum to his brother's heirs.

The existence of Lee's lost silver mine near the Old Woman Springs continued to plague Waterman, and the politician never gave up searching for it. In 1886, he employed two men to explore the area for him and try to find the mine. In the meantime, Waterman ran for the office of lieutenant governor of the state of California and won. A year later, Governor Bartlett died and Waterman ascended to that office. Though burdened with running the state of California, Waterman never relinquished his passion for locating Lee's secret mine, and before he died in 1892, he maintained a standing offer of one-half interest in the mine to anyone who could locate it for him.

Several years later, map-makers applied the name Old Woman Springs to a group of freshwater springs actually located several miles from where George C. Lee was murdered. The location of the original site of Old Woman Springs is questionable, but if it were ever accurately identified, it could serve as a starting place for a search for Lee's lost silver mine.

The Lost Treasure Ship
of the California Desert

FOR CENTURIES THE VAST, ARID, and undulating landscape that comprises the desert country of southern California was largely avoided by humans and animals alike. The lack of water and vegetation along with the unending stretches of windblown sands studded by remote rocky outcrops discouraged all but the most savage, the hopelessly lost, or the eternally optimistic prospectors and miners who entered the region and hammered away at the exposed granites in search of precious metals.

This sparse and sere desert that straddles the border separating California from the Mexican state of Baja California Norte is not only dangerous and forbidding but also endowed with an aura of mystery, and one of its greatest mysteries is that associated with a centuries-old, treasure-laden ocean vessel believed to be resting in the ever-shifting sands somewhere near the center of this remote land.

When migrants from the southern and eastern states encountered this desert while traveling to the fertile and promising coastal lands that lay to the west during the eighteenth and nineteenth centuries, they shuddered at the task that lay before them—the multi-day crossing of this treeless and waterless waste. Many died along the way, but most survived, and among the survivors were several who reported seeing a masted Spanish galleon partially buried in the glimmering dunes. Several returned to the area in an attempt to relocate the mysterious ship, but it remained elusive, presumably hidden by the constantly shifting sands of the desert. Anyone lucky enough to have found the ancient ship, however, would have been rewarded with the fortune of an empire, for over 250 years earlier, millions of dollars' worth of exquisite pearls were neatly stored in the hold of the vessel in several large wooden chests.

The tale of the lost treasure ship of the southern California desert had its beginnings in 1610. In that year, Philip III, the reigning King of Spain, ordered Alvarez de Cordone, a loyal captain stationed in Mexico City, to arrange for an expedition along the western coast of Mexico in search of pearls. During this time, pearls were considered by many to be more precious than gold or silver, and the king was anxious to fill the treasury of his country with the great wealth he believed could be found in this new land in the western hemisphere.

According to his instructions, Cordone was to supervise the construction of three ships and have them properly outfitted for the expedition. After appointing two additional captains—Juan de Iturbe and Pedro de Rosales—the three men, accompanied by an armed escort, proceeded to the coastal village of Acapulco, some 250 miles to the south. While the ships were being constructed, Cordone requested the importation of sixty experienced pearl divers from Africa.

In July of 1612, the three vessels were finally declared seaworthy, and Cordone led the expedition into the Pacific waters and on a northwesterly course paralleling the Mexican shore.

Cordone, like many Spanish explorers of the time, knew that this part of the Pacific Ocean was home to a relatively large mollusk that was capable of producing an impressive pearl of a desirable, dark hue and a shiny, almost metallic, surface. Such pearls were prized by wealthy Europeans, and King Philip hoped to supply enough to those who had the price to pay for them.

As the three ships lazily plied the calm coastal waters, occasional stops were ordered so that the divers could explore and harvest the oyster beds encountered along the way. While some pearls were found, they accumulated much too slowly to satisfy Cordone. He knew that the richest beds were located far to the northwest in the Gulf of California, and it was to this region he directed his ships.

After several days of sailing, the Spaniards encountered a large Indian village located on the shore and observed that some of the men were also diving for pearls in the shallow coastal waters. Believing he might find some fine specimens among those accumulated by the Indians, Cordone ordered the anchors dropped and he, escorted by several crewmen, put ashore to converse with the village chieftain.

Although the Spaniards were the first white men ever encountered by the Indians, the newcomers were greeted warmly and provided with food and lodging. Using signs and gestures, Cordone and the chief conversed throughout much of the night and the following day. Eventually, the Spanish captain inquired about the pearls and was informed that the Indians harvested the oysters principally for food, and when a pearl was found it was stored with others and saved for those who fashioned necklaces and other adornments. When Cordone asked if he could see the pearls, he was surprised and delighted to be shown over two dozen clay pots filled to the top with the finest stones he had ever seen.

When Cordone asked the chief if he would like to trade the pearls for some clothes such as those worn by the Spaniards, the Indian readily agreed and looked forward to garbing himself in such finery as worn by those who stood before him. An agreement was made and Cordone, along with his escort, returned to the ships.

The next morning several neatly tied bundles of clothing were deposited on the shore in exchange for the pots filled with pearls. As the precious stones were being transferred to the hold of Iturbe's ship, the Indians on the shore raised a howl and gestured angrily at the Spaniards. After untying the bundles, they discovered they had traded away their collection of stones for little more than discarded rags and worn out clothing. Enraged, several of the warriors waded far out into he surf and launched arrows toward the ships. As Cordone ordered the sails hoisted and the ships under way, an arrow struck him in the chest, felling him instantly. As the expedition's surgeon fussed over the Spanish leader, the vessels sailed safely away from the shore.

The next day found Cordone in great pain and suffering as a result of his wound. Convinced that the captain had contracted blood poisoning, the physician recommended he return at once to Acapulco where he could be properly treated. Otherwise, he informed Cordone, he would most certainly die. Before departing, Cordone instructed Iturbe and Rosales to continue up the the coast into the Gulf of California to harvest more pearls. There, he told them, they would find the breeding ground of the pearl-bearing oysters they sought.

When the two remaining galleons arrived in the gulf several weeks later, the Spaniards were delighted to discover many rich mollusk beds yielding numerous gleaming pearls. As the divers gathered this incredible wealth from the ocean shelf, Iturbe and Rosales formulated plans to continue farther north in the hope of finding even larger oyster beds near the point where the gulf constricts and accepts the outflow from the Colorado River. Both officers believed that if they returned to port with a huge cargo of fine pearls far exceeding the expectations of Cordone and the king, they would be rewarded with promotions and important assignments in the Atlantic. The growing lust for military status manifested by the two captains was to prove their undoing, however, for one day as Rosales's ship, already heavy with pearls, glided through the waters just off the coast of Isla Angel de la Guardia, it struck a reef which tore a great hole in the oaken hull. As the ship slowly settled into the blue waters of the gulf, the crewmen worked frantically transferring its rich cargo onto the remaining vessel.

Following a conference, Iturbe and Rosales decided to continue to sail the remaining ship even farther north in search of more oyster beds, though the hull of Iturbe's galleon already contained several large chests filled with the magnificent stones.

Several days later the lone ship entered the estuarine waters where the Colorado River met the gulf. During this time, the river carried a greater amount of water than it does today, and the flow spilled nearly sixty miles from the channel into the basin-shaped desert lowlands to the west, forming a huge inland sea. Into this body of water sailed Iturbe's ship, the Spaniards and African divers constantly in search of more oyster beds.

For two weeks the party explored the inland sea and found it to be nothing more than a shallow accumulation of overflow from the river. Determined to return to the gulf, Iturbe navigated the vessel to the point where they entered this body of water only to discover a low ridge of land separating it from the riverine outlet. The galleon was hopelessly landlocked!

Geologists have since surmised that an earthquake likely occurred during this time, causing a sudden subtle shifting of the continental plate, creating a change in the topography of this region, and shifting the Colorado River several miles eastward. This low desert region of California actually straddles the San Andreas fault, North America's most active earthquake region, and tremors here are commonplace.

Determined to find another route to the gulf, Iturbe once again sailed around the shallow sea only to return to the same point several days later. Not only was the ship trapped a hundred miles from the gulf, but due to the intense evaporation that was taking place along with the fact that the Colorado River no longer supplied any water, the level of the sea was lowering at a rapid rate. Several days later, the bottom of the ship's hull became lodged on the sandy bottom and started listing to one side as the waters receded.

Realizing the ship was permanently mired in the soft bottom, the crew, with no other choice facing them, gathered what they could carry and struck out across the drying sandy plain toward the gulf. Four months later, the survivors were picked up by a Spanish vessel near the present-day coastal town of Guaymas.

As the rescued Spaniards and divers were being transported to Acapulco, hundreds of miles to the north the masted galleon formerly under Iturbe's command rested at a severe angle on the now dry desert landscape, its sails mere tatters from the constant buffeting of the wind. On the windward side of the ship, drifting sand had accumulated nearly to the gunwales and threatened to cover the hull in the coming months. Deep within the large hold, a fortune in fine pearls reposed in wooden chests now lightly covered with a fine desert dust.

For over two centuries the treasure-filled galleon lay on the desert floor, sometimes covered and other times exposed by the sand-shifting winds.

Following the Civil War, thousands of citizens began migrating from the battle-scarred south to the California coast and passed through this arid expanse of southern California now known as the Colorado Desert. Many encountered a strange phenomena—the remains of a Spanish sailing ship resting on the desert floor, its masts poking heavenward. For decades, hundreds of such sightings were reported throughout southern California.

Years passed, and as the true story of the Spanish treasure ship became known, numerous expeditions entered the desert in search of it. In spite of the many well-organized quests, the vessel could not be found. Some claimed it never existed, but the historical record is clear. Others claimed it was buried under the desert sands. Still others claimed the vessel was haunted and appeared only at certain times of the year.

During the 1880s several prospectors on different occasions walked out of the Colorado Desert into adjacent settlements claiming they had seen a ship, but due to lack of water or provisions none were able to investigate it. One old-timer even claimed to have camped for several days inside the slowly rotting hull of the old galleon but he was unaware of the existence of the huge store of pearls stored inside, presumably under many feet of sand by now. Years later when he was informed of the huge fortune he missed, the old man returned to the region but was unable to relocate the vessel.

In 1892, a party of prospectors, traveling near Superstition Mountain, discovered a long mast timber lying on the desert floor partially covered by drifting sand. One of the members of the party was familiar with the tale of the treasure ship and encouraged the others to search for it. Though they explored the immediate area for the next two days, nothing could be found, and they surmised the ship was buried under one of the huge dunes that dominated the landscape.

In 1915, an aged Yuma Indian arrived at the town of Indio and attempted to purchase food with a handful of small shiny round stones. When a local businessman realized that the stones were actually pearls he asked the Indian where he found them. In a long and rambling explanation, the old man spoke of a great journey he recently made across the desert and finding a strangely shaped "wooden house" partially covered by sand. Inside the house, he stated, he discovered "many wooden cases which contained thousands of the small round rose- and cream-colored stones."

Excited, a small group of Indio citizens offered the old Indian several hundred dollars if he would lead them to the "wooden house." He agreed, was paid, and accepted an invitation to lodge that night at the home of one of the investors. In the morning, however, the Indian had vanished and was never seen again.

Even today, backpackers, hunters, and trail bikers return from the interior of the Colorado Desert with stories of finding an exposed bow or stern of an old ship. Most are intrigued when they learn of the circumstances which brought Iturbe's vessel to this remote part of California, and all are amazed when informed of the great fortune in pearls reported to be stored in the hold of the ancient ship.

Someday the ever-changing desert winds will once again uncover the mysterious treasure ship, and perhaps this time some fortunate hiker or prospector may discover the store of pearls within, pearls that today would equal the combined wealth of several countries.

Pothole Gold

STORIES OF ABANDONED SPANISH MINES abound throughout the deserts of Southern California. Part fact and part folklore, these stories serve as a strong lure to many who dream of wealth. One such mine located not far from the Arizona border has been found and lost on numerous occasions.

Around 1880, several Mexicans arrived in the area of El Centro, California with an old map purportedly showing the location of a rich mine near a region north of Winterhaven and not far from the Colorado River known as the Potholes. For several years, the Mexicans remained in the Potholes, constructed several adobe and rock huts, and apparently extracted gold ore from a nearby shaft. Every three or four months, two of the Mexicans would travel to Yuma, Arizona, to exchange the ore for cash and to purchase food and supplies. Those who engaged in transactions with the Mexicans claim the gold was of the purest quality and there appeared to be plenty of it. When the Mexicans were asked about the location of their mine, they remained secretive and hurried out of town.

The location in the desert where the Mexicans lived was given the name Picacho after a nearby peak, but the site was mysteriously abandoned around 1890. A short time later, a party of miners from Arizona moved into the area to prospect for ore and opened several mines. Before the turn of the century, their diggings, located just north of the present-day Yuma Indian Reservation, were highly productive and yielded approximately $50,000 per month. While evidence of early Spanish settlement was often encountered by the miners throughout the area, the original Spanish mine was never found. Eventually the Picacho mines were exhausted and abandoned.

During the summer of 1910, two aged Yuma Indians walked into a supply store in the town of El Centro, gathered a mound of canned goods and other supplies on the store counter, and offered the clerk a handful of nuggets of almost pure gold as payment.

Unused to this medium of exchange and unable to converse in the language of the Indians, the store clerk summoned an area old-timer known to have lived for many years among the Yumas. After negotiating the purchase of the goods, the old man asked the two Indians where they had obtained the gold. One of the Yumas pointed to the west across the river and mentioned an old Spanish mine known to his tribe and found in the Potholes region.

Intrigued, the old man later traveled to the Potholes to search for the mine but was never able to locate it. The story of the gold brought in by the Indians soon spread throughout the area and was picked up by newspapers, and soon treasure hunters and prospectors arrived from as far away as Indiana to search for the mysterious mine. For years, hundreds of people searched for it only to find disappointment and sometimes death. The waterless landscape, devoid of shelter from the blinding sunshine, with summer surface temperatures in excess of 170 degrees, claimed several lives.

In 1918, a physician from Yuma named DeCoursey learned the story of the abandoned Spanish gold mine in the Potholes area as a result of studying church archives in Mexico City. On returning to the United States, DeCoursey interviewed several elderly Yuma Indians and found one who was familiar with the tale. The Indian related an intriguing story about the productive mine, the enslavement of his kinsman by missionaries, and a subsequent Indian uprising which ultimately drove out the hated Spaniards. During the interview, DeCoursey was pleased to discover that the old man claimed to know the exact location of the mine at the Potholes.

After agreeing to guide the physician to the mine, the Indian arranged for the purchase of horses and supplies, and early one morning the two rode out into the desert. During the long journey to the Potholes, the Indian told DeCoursey that, because so many Yumas died in the mine while enslaved by the Spaniards, a curse was placed on it, a curse which held that any member of the tribe who entered the shaft or showed another where it was located was destined to die. When DeCoursey asked the old Indian if he was bothered by the curse, the Yuma merely looked away, not answering, but as the two men neared the Potholes, the Indian grew increasingly nervous.

While DeCoursey and the Yuma were still several miles from the alleged location of the mine, the Indian pointed to a distant ridge and told the physician that the shaft was located not far from it. With that, he turned his horse and rode back toward Yuma. DeCoursey spent the next two weeks roaming about the area in search of the old abandoned shaft but was unsuccessful. When he returned to town, DeCoursey was unable to get the Indian to speak about the mine anymore.

In 1925, a stranger arrived in Yuma and dumped a small leather sack full of gold nuggets onto the crude plank bar of a local tavern. To those who inquired, he explained that he had dug the gold out of an old mine shaft he found in the Potholes region. During subsequent months, the stranger, who claimed he was originally from Oregon, was often seen walking out of the desert from the west and arriving at the river town carrying one or more sacks filled with gold ore. This went on for nearly a year, but the stranger eventually stopped coming and was never seen again. His discovery of gold, however, spurred renewed efforts to locate the mine, and once again dozens of adventurous men searched the Potholes area for the rich deposit. None have claimed discovery, but the chances that this mine actually existed and may still contain a rich vein of gold are excellent.

Many aspects of these tales have been validated by scholarly research. Studies undertaken during the past several decades have revealed that, during the early stages of Spanish settlement in California, several productive gold and silver mines were opened and operated. During the seventeenth centuries, Spanish missionaries virtually enslaved local Indians and forced them to extract the ore which was then shipped by pack train to Mexico City. Near the end of the seventeenth century, however, the Indians revolted and drove the Spaniards from the region, and many of the highly productive mines were simply abandoned. One such mine, according to the research, was reputed to be located near the Potholes region of southeastern California.

Today, people still enter this rugged region in search of the old, abandoned Spanish mine. Individuals occasionally return to Yuma, as did prospectors of long ago, with small amounts of gold they managed to find in the area, but the original shaft, apparently still containing a vein of rich gold, continues to elude researchers.

Hill of Black Gold

IN THE COLORADO DESERT of southern California lies a low, rounded hill littered with thousands of small black stones. The stones, which are gold nuggets coated with a thin layer of manganese, were discovered in 1829 by a colorful western character named Pegleg Smith. To this day, Smith's hill of "black gold" remains one of California's most elusive lost treasures.

Thomas L. Smith was a hunter, trapper, explorer, and scout during most of the first thirty years of the nineteenth century. A contemporary of noted frontiersmen Jim Bridger, Bill Williams, and Kit Carson, Smith had trapped beaver throughout most of the Rocky Mountain West and was a veteran of dozens of Indian fights. During one such skirmish, Smith's shin bone was shattered by a bullet. The useless limb was badly in need of amputation and, when none of his companions were willing to attempt it, Smith cut off his own leg below the knee with a large skinning knife. With the same knife, he later carved a wooden stump which he attached to what was left of his lower leg and was thereafter known as Pegleg Smith. The injury and subsequent handicap did not diminish his enthusiasm for trapping and he continued to range the wilderness for many more years, always searching for the ideal beaver stream until the demand for beaver pelts began to plummet.

In 1829, Pegleg Smith was contracted by a fur company to guide a party of trappers into southern Utah and northern Arizona in search of some promising streams. Unfortunately, the group met with disappointment as most of the streams had been trapped out. After exploring the area around the Bill Williams River in western Arizona, the party decided to disband. With his friend Maurice LeDoux, Smith decided to travel southward to Yuma and then cut across the desert in southern California to San Diego. Smith had seen few deserts, and was unprepared for the hostile environment he entered after leaving Yuma. Once leaving the flood plain of the Colorado River, the two men encountered little more than high winds and hostile Indians.

On the afternoon of the third day of the trek, a severe sandstorm reduced visibility to only a few feet. The storm lasted for three days and when it finally let up, the two men discovered they had strayed far from the trail they intended to follow. Smith and LeDoux, though extremely competent mountain men, were out of their element in the harsh desert. Grudgingly, they admitted they were lost. And they were also almost out of water.

One evening as the two travelers prepared to camp in the lee side of a large sand dune, Smith decided to explore the immediate area in an attempt to get his bearings and to try to locate a spring. While LeDoux prepared dinner, Smith regarded with interest three low hills rising from the desert floor about a mile from their camp. The middle hill was the tallest of the three, and Smith decided to climb to the top and survey the region. As he hobbled toward the trio of knolls, Smith also noticed that the center one was much darker in color than the others.

While climbing to the top of the hill, Smith noticed the surface was littered with small, black stones ranging from the size of a grape to that of a walnut. He picked up a handful and discovered they were quite heavy. As Smith scanned the horizons, he absent-mindedly placed a handful of the stones into one of his pockets.

Following dinner that evening, Smith pulled one of the black stones from his pocket and proceeded to scape away the surface crust with his knife. To his surprise, he discovered a brightly colored and somewhat malleable core just beneath the dark coating. Believing it was copper, Smith suggested to his companion that they might be able to make some bullets out of the rocks sometime in the future.

About two weeks later, Smith and LeDoux straggled into a small settlement on the outskirts of Los Angeles where they watered themselves and their stock and rested for a few days before proceeding on to the coast. While camping here, Smith pulled one of the heavy stones from his pocket and showed it to one of the settlers. The farmer laughed at Smith's assertion that it was copper, carefully removed the thin layer of manganese that coated each of the nuggets, and informed him he was in the possession of some very rich gold ore.

Though he believed the settler's assessment that the stones were almost pure gold, Smith was unimpressed with the information. The mountain man continued to believe a fortune could made with furs and was not swayed by the prospect that he might become a rich man by mining gold. In addition, Smith's discovery of the gold-littered hill was twenty years prior to the great California gold rush and he was completely unaware of the significance of his find.

After arriving in Los Angeles, Smith and LeDoux parted company. For several years the old mountain man drifted from one business venture to another, all the while believing that the demand for fur would return. While he longed to go back to his beloved Rocky Mountains, he continued to place his hopes in a resurgence of demand for beaver pelts. As time passed, Smith remained relatively content with his lot in southern California. While he never grew wealthy, he lived a comfortable life.

When gold was discovered at Sutter's Mill and the California gold rush of 1849 was on, Smith was awed at the incredible fortunes that were made in a matter of a few days. Suddenly realizing how easily gold could make a millionaire out of a pauper, the former trapper began to reconsider his twenty-year-old discovery of the manganese-encrusted gold nuggets on the low knoll somewhere in the Colorado Desert. Believing he would have no trouble relocating the knoll where he found the gold, Smith organized a small party of miners and led an expedition from Los Angeles to the uninhabited arid wastes near the Mexican border.

Once in the desert, however, Smith became disoriented and could identify none of the landmarks he thought he remembered. Discouraged, the group returned to San Diego. Smith immediately thought to contact his old friend LeDoux, believing that together the two would be able to retrace their route to the three knolls. For several weeks Smith searched for his partner only to discover he had died in San Diego several years earlier.

Smith continued his determination to return to the desert and relocate the gold he knew existed in great quantities atop the low hill. By 1854, he had organized another expedition to go into the desert to search. Smith's descriptions of the three knolls and the abundance of gold that could be found were so convincing that several members of the expedition agreed to finance it for a large share of the profits once gold was discovered.

For several weeks the party ranged throughout the desert between Mexicali and Yuma and northward toward the Chocolate Mountains. On several occasions clusters of small hills appeared on the horizon, but on closer investigation none of them yielded any gold whatsoever.

Smith pursued his quest to find the lost gold in the southern California desert until around 1860. With gold still plentiful in northern California, no one cared to venture into the waterless tract of the lower desert. By this time, Smith had become a heavy drinker and earned a reputation for being unreliable. Sadly, Thomas L. Smith, known as Pegleg, died a pauper in San Francisco in 1866.

The story of the Lost Pegleg Mine, as Smith's gold came

to be called, had almost faded from the memory of most Californians when it was apparently discovered about ten years following the old trapper's death. Sometime around 1876, an elderly prospector who was trying his luck in the Colorado Desert chanced upon three knolls located several miles north of the east-west trail that connects Yuma with San Diego. Because he was familiar with the story of the Lost Pegleg Mine, the prospector decided to investigate and was rewarded with the discovery of thousands of black-coated gold nuggets scattered all over the middle hill. He packed all the nuggets he could carry onto his burro and walked into Yuma where he converted the ore into thousands of dollars in cash. As the old prospector was preparing for a return trip to the mysterious knoll, he fell ill and died.

During the first decade of the twentieth century, a pair of Indians walked into the settlement of Brawley and tried to purchase some goods with several gold nuggets. The owner of the mercantile examined the gold closely and discovered what remained of a thin coating of manganese on each of them. As he was familiar with the tale of the Lost Pegleg Mine, he asked the Indians where they found the gold, but the two men only provided vague answers about a hill covered with them and pointed out toward the desert. The next day the two Indians disappeared and were never seen again.

It is rare that gold nuggets are found with a coating of manganese about them. It is remarkable that Smith, the old prospector, and the two Indians who appeared in Brawley indicated they had found a hill literally covered with them. In each of the three cases, the gold, when assayed, was reported to be extremely rich.

There are portions of the Colorado Desert of southern California that are quite remote and distant from well traveled highways and population centers. That such a hill covered with gold can exist and not be located seems impossible in an age of high-technological mapping and surveillance gear. But one cannot fully appreciate the vastness, the emptiness, and the remoteness of this great desert until one has traveled the old trails once walked and ridden by the old prospectors of the last century. Each year, people enter the heart of this desert wilderness. Some of them are in search of recreation, backpacking, and trail-biking. Some still come in search of the Lost Pegleg Mine. Each year a few of these people become lost and search parties are sent out to locate them. Most of them are found, but occasionally some are not. A search and rescue team member once stated that even with countless helicopters, planes, four-wheelers, maps, and tracking dogs at their disposal, most of the lost are located by pure luck.

So it may be with Pegleg Smith's hill of black gold.

Selected References

Bean, Walton. *California: An Interpretive History* (New York: McGraw-Hill Publishing Co., 1968).

Billington, Ray A. (Ed.). *The Gold Mines of California* (New York: Arno Press, 1973).

Borthwick, J.D. *The Gold Hunters* (Ann Arbor, Michigan: Gryphon Books, 1971).

Buffum, Edward Gould. *Six Months in the Gold Mines* (Ann Arbor, Michigan: University Microfilms, Inc., 1966).

Caughey, John Walton. *Gold is the Cornerstone* (Berkeley: University of California Press, 1948).

Chalfant, W.A. *Death Valley* (Stanford, California: Stanford University Press, 1930).

Chapman, Charles E. *A History of California: the Spanish Period* (New York: The MacMillan Company, 1921).

Clark, Howard D. *Lost Mines of the Old West* (Los Angeles: Ghost Town Press. 1946).

Cleland, Robert Glass. *From Wilderness to Empire* (New York: Alfred A. Knopf, 1949).

Conrotto, Eugene. *Lost Desert Bonanzas* (Palm Desert, California: Desert-Southwest Publishers, 1963).

Dobie, J. Frank. *Coronado's Children* (Austin: University of Texas Press. 1978).

Edwards, Harold L. "A Bloody Yarn: The Story of John Schipe's Lost Mine," *True West,* July, 1992.

Hunt, Rockwell D., and Van de Grift Sanchez, Nellie. *A Short History of California* (New York: Thomas Y. Crowell Company, 1929).

Hutchinson, W.H. *California: Two Centuries of Man, Land, and Growth in the Golden State* (Palo Alto, California: American West Publishing Company, 1969).

Irons, Angie. "Rattlesnake Dick's Lost Gold Caches," *Lost Treasure*, August, 1990.

Jackson, Joseph Henry. *Gold Rush Album* (New York: Charles Scribner's Sons, 1949).

Jaeger, Edmund C. *The Calfornia Deserts* (Stanford, California: Stanford University Press, 1931).

Jameson, W.C. "The Lost Harding Silver," *Lost Treasure*, November, 1992.

Jameson, W.C. "The Lost Gold Nugget Spring," *Lost Treasure*. September, 1992.

Johnson, W.G. *Experiences of a Forty-niner* (New York: Arno Press, 1973).

Johnson, William Weber. *The Forty-niners* (New York: Time-Life Books, 1974).

Latham, John H. *Famous Lost Mines of the Old West* (Conroe, Texas: True Treasure Publications, Inc., 1971).

Leeper, David Rohrer. *The Argonauts of Forty-nine* (South Bend, Indiana: J.B. Stoll and Company, 1894).

LeGaye, E.S. *Treasure Anthology* (Houston, Texas: Western Heritage Press. 1973).

Lovelace, Leland. *Lost Mines and Hidden Treasure* (San Antonio, Texas: The Naylor Company, 1956).

Marryat, Frank. *Mountains and Molehills* (London: Longman, Brown, Green, and Longman, 1855).

Masters, Al. "Amazing Treasure Ship of the California Desert," *Lost Treasure*, July, 1977.

Mitchell, John D. *Lost Mines of the Great Southwest* (Phoenix: The Journal Co., Inc. 1933).

Paul, Rodman W. *California Gold* (Lincoln: University of Nebraska Press, 1947).

Perlot, Jean-Nicolas. *Gold Seekers* (New Haven, Connecticut: Yale University Press, 1985).

Powell, John J. *The Golden State and Its Resources* (San Francisco: Bacon and Company, 1874).

Rascoe, Jesse. *Southern California Treaures* (Fort Davis, Texas: Frontier Book Company, 1969).

Read, Georgia Willis, and Gaines, Ruth (Eds.). *Gold Rush* (New York: Columbia University Press, 1949).

Shinn, Charles Howard. *Mining Camps* (New York: Harper and Row, Publishers, 1965).

Weight, Harold O. *Lost Mines of Death Valley* (Twenty-nine Palms, California: The Calico Press, 1953).

Weinman, Ken. "The Boozer's Lost Cache of Gold," *Lost Treasure*, August, 1990.

Williams, Brad and Pepper, Choral. *Lost Treaures of the West* (New York: Holt, Rinehart, and Winston, 1975).

Williams, Carlos. "The Golden Spring of the Salmon River Mountains," *Lost Treasure*, November, 1992.